Lucy Mushita is a novelist, essayist and speaker. Born in Zimbabwe, she grew up in a traditional village before going to France at the end of apartheid. After a short stay in the USA she went back to France where she taught English in primary school, at university and to multinational executives. With a University of Sydney MA in Creative Writing, Lucy writes full time and lives between France and Australia. She is published in English, Italian, French and other languages.

Chinongwa

LUCY MUSHITA

SPINIFEX

We respectfully acknowledge the wisdom of Aboriginal and Torres Strait Islander peoples and their custodianship of the lands and waterways. Spinifex offices are located on Djiru, Bunurong, Wadawurrung, Eora, and Noongar Country.

Published in conjunction with Weaver Press, Zimbabwe and Modjaji Books, South Africa. Published by both these independent publishers in 2022.

First published by Spinifex Press, 2023
Spinifex Press Pty Ltd
PO Box 200, Little River, VIC 3211, Australia
PO Box 105, Mission Beach, QLD 4852, Australia

women@spinifexpress.com.au
www.spinifexpress.com.au

Edited by Susan Hawthorne, Pauline Hopkins and Renate Klein
Cover design by Deb Snibson
Typesetting by Helen Christie, Blue Wren Books
Typeset in Albertina
Printed in the USA

A catalogue record for this book is available from the National Library of Australia

ISBN: 9781925950816 (paperback)
ISBN: 9781925950823 (ebook)

To Tapiwa & Anika

ACKNOWLEDGEMENTS

Mother, thank you for providing the four corners of stability that have allowed me to withstand gale-force winds and storms, swollen rivers and rough oceans. When lost, all I need is to stand still, close my eyes and listen to your voice.

Father, our own clown, thank you for giving us the giggles; I am still laughing. But most of all, thank you for balancing that bucket of water on your head like a woman. Though then I cringed as I watched the village laughing at you, now I know you were the most manly of them all.

To Augustine, Mike, Andrew and Aquilina, you are the best siblings and buddies.

To Sister-in-Crime Kidi Bebey, English temptress Vanessa White, plucky American Susan Russick, French adventurous woman Nathalie Moalic, kick-ass Aussie businesswoman Christine Metcalfe and *femme d'affaire redoubtable* Fréderique Doumic, thank you all for the cocooning.

To my literary agent Raphaël Thierry of Ægitna Literary Agency, thank you for your unwavering support and constant encouragement.

To American writer Jake Lamar, thank you for finding me.

To the literary virtuoso Bernard Magnier, thank you for believing in me.

To Niasha, thank you Dr Hobbes for being in my life, keep healing.

To Tendai, thank you word spinner for being in my life, keep scribbling.

To Rose and Chloé, welcome to the girls' club; you are awesome.

To my Aussie hunk Blundell, thank you for carrying the suitcases.

Last but not least, thanks to the French government for providing relatively free education and subsidised balanced meals from pre-school to university. I was able to listen to the voices in my head and write this book from 8 a.m. to 4.30 p.m., four days a week.

CHRONOLOGY

1855	Sekuru Marehwa is born
1871	Baba Chitsva is born
1882	Baba Marehwa is born
1906	Wangi is born
1908	Tawa is born
1910	Chinongwa is born
1919	Chinongwa marries
1921	First boy-child dies after weeks
1922	Tinashe, boy, is born
1924	Tendai, boy, is born
1925	Stillbirth, girl, after singing
1925	Amaiguru leaves
1926	Nyasha, girl, is born
1928	Rumbi, girl, is born
1930	Tagarika, girl, dies at two
1932	Chido, girl, is born
1934	Tatenda, the last boy, is born
1935	Baba Chitsva dies
1936	Chinongwa is sent away
1937	Chikomborero, the girl from rape, is born
1940	Chinongwa is telling all

BOOK 1

1

Chinongwa Marehwa was nine, but her age was not vital, just her virginity. Though she was not yet washing, her fruits were already protruding. That was a relief for her family. Anyway, she was the only one they could use.

"Your sister was even younger when she was given," Ambuya never missed an occasion to tell her. It was supposed to make her feel more fortunate than her older sister, Muraswa, but the words made her push her ear lobes into the holes, a trick she used to block out unwelcome sounds like owls hooting or snoring; but she could only do this when there was nobody around except her blind maternal grandmother.

Chinongwa remembered that two summers after Muraswa was promised, her betrothed had come with his clan trailing behind to claim what belonged to him. As far as Chinongwa was concerned, Muraswa had then disappeared from the face of the earth into the bushes behind their compound. For some time afterwards, whenever she heard that a young girl had been married off, she imagined her disappearing into the undergrowth; with stoical indifference, she waited for her turn to come.

She didn't recall whether or not she had cried for Muraswa with the other clan women. The only details engraved in her memory were the disproportionately thick-veined hands and fingers of her sister's husband-to-be, the heavy silence punctuated by sniffs every now and then in the smoke-filled hut, while the Marehwa women went about cooking. Then, after their two-day stay, the procession of the future husband's family disappearing behind the thatched huts. She could still see Muraswa, who did not turn once to look back at her home and people, shuffling in front of one of those broad-backed and thick-calved women. For many moons, Chinongwa would quietly chant, "Dzoka Muraswa, dzoka,"[1] while staring at the bushes that had swallowed her sister.

As expected, Mai Marehwa did not eat for days on end after Muraswa's departure. Ambuya came to preach sense into her, "You're not the first woman whose daughter has been given away. There's worse that could happen. Don't shed tears as if she were dead. If her womb doesn't produce because you've filled it with your tears, that old midget of hers will return her and demand his food back. What will you do then? Have you not turned his millet into shit already?"

Mai Marehwa did not answer or get off the mat she was lying on in the dark cooking hut. She kept her eyes shut so as not to look into her mother's face for fear they would both cry. She coughed to acknowledge that she was paying attention.

Her mother continued, "Don't forget that Chinongwa and your sons don't care how much you suffer; they only want you to know how they feel. And, just as well, otherwise all mothers would starve themselves to death. A woman is the central pole of the world and

---

1   A glossary can be found on pages 233 to 235.

that means carrying one's load with pride, at least for the sake of your children."

As expected, village women came by to force-feed her until the mourning period was over and, thinner than ever, she started to swallow a mouthful or two to 'keep her strength for the other children.'

Baba Marehwa complained about his wife's amazing behaviour. "We have given our daughter away so that we can eat, no? Now look at her, enough millet in the granary for the next four moons, and she is refusing to eat. I know she suffers. Do I not suffer too? Had I had a choice, would I have given a product of my own loins to some unknown small, vulgar villain older than myself?"

His younger brother had soothing words, "A woman is like a hen. Unlike a cock that understands the situation instantly and goes to hide under the chicken barn, a hen cackles as if demented and blows her wings in pursuit of that eagle that has come to pluck her chicks away. As if unaware that the eagle could end the hen's life there and then. And then what would happen to the other chicks? Is it not better, if one has no choice, to sacrifice one and save ten, as the saying goes? But then women think with their hearts. Unlike us, they have no brains."

Baba Marehwa did not answer, but the other men sitting in the tree shade at the dare, passing around the clay beer pot from one to the other, grunted in agreement. Encouraged, the younger brother went on. "Even when her daughter marries the boy she has always wanted for her, and she receives the fattest cow and most beautiful cloth—enough for two dresses and one for each of her three sisters—the night the groom comes to claim her daughter, the mother, with the new dress on and aware that the whole village is admiring her, will cry and tear her hair. And yet her heart beats fast for the grandchildren that are going to come out of the womb from her own womb. That woman who does not cry but celebrates her daughter's departure by killing a fat pig and eating it with red millet sadza, has not yet been born." Here, the whole dare broke into laughter.

No one had ever sat Chinongwa down to tell her that she was going to be given away, but she was neither deaf nor blind. The trees knew it and whispered, gossiped and laughed about it all day, all night. The grass knew it, and during the dry season kept the secret in its roots so as to pass it on to the delicate shoots that sprouted after the first rains. When she looked at the cows staring at her while they ruminated, she saw the pity in their eyes because they knew that she was nothing but a girl who was going to be given away. She shied away from them and pretended she did not see their huge, wide eyes and the tears they shed for her. When she went to watch out for the baboons and monkeys, the baboons ignored her as if out of shame, and the monkeys mocked her.

Of her father's three sisters, Chinongwa knew that two were given away for food and cattle. They ate the food and used the cattle to marry off her father's younger brother. She had met one of those aunts but could not remember where or when. The third aunt, Shorai, who lived a stone's throw away from them, got married for love at the ripe age of five and ten.

Chinongwa did not find it amiss that she did not like her two older aunts. They did not like her father. What troubled her was her loathing of Shorai. Because Shorai got on with her parents, she had to feign liking her. She suspected her aunt of being purposely unlovable, but how could she be sure? Perhaps she begrudged Shorai for marrying for love, while Muraswa was given away— as she would be.

So, every day Chinongwa waited and searched for him to whom she was to be given. Every male who crossed her path, young or old, was a potential husband, and she silently and secretly scrutinised his face. At night, while she stared at the dying fire in the cooking hut where she slept, she made the day file past for analysis. Had a husband crossed her way? Had she understood all the words she had heard today, all the scents? That handshake, had it been innocent? She had to be the first to know.

She was skeptical when she listened to the adults going on and on about how rich they used to be before the removals. Her father never tired of saying, "Four or more granaries to a family and you should have seen how much those granaries overflowed with all kinds of millet. And game, even women were able to catch hares with their woven baskets. Men with short legs did not have to chase animals but threw their spears randomly and came home with an animal strung across the shoulder. Long-legged men brought in kudus or buffalo."

Ambuya was more interested in how juicy girls used to be, especially herself. "A girl of three and ten summers was already fully grown, and I was fully grown even before that. My calves, thighs and buttocks shone with the juice that was inside me, when I oiled them. Men held wrestling matches to decide who would marry me. And we were married right away. Today's girls are like today's cattle, dried up: just bones covered with stretched skin."

Though Chinongwa knew she was thin, she bore no grudge and got carried away imagining herself a time of plenty, when girls were glowingly nubile, land was there for all, and people's pens overflowed with cattle lowing to be milked. Good times, when parents of brides got all their cows for roora in one day before delivering the bride. Repossession of daughters for cows unpaid was unheard of. But at times Chinongwa found it hard to differentiate between such reminiscences and the fables the elders recounted in the evenings after the harvest. Both held a hint of romance and fantasy. She had never seen talking lions or singing pythons that gave their eggs to humans but then, neither had she ever seen overflowing granaries, rivers of milk and honey, nor vasinamabvi, the kneeless, with a woman king.

To get some sense out of this jumble, she decided that all that was happy and fantastic was made up. Reality was their king who had sold their land to a woman king. The evidence was in the steady flow of beggarly families who came through the village. Sometimes they drove a bony cow or two. Some were received with tears of joy and the little patch of rocky land was once more divided. Others, who had no relatives or close family in the village, were reluctantly received and fed for a few days while they rested their feet before being encouraged to the next village. Chinongwa could not close her eyes to that, though she drew a line where the woman king was concerned. "Women cannot be kings. Who has ever seen her?"

She felt no relief when Ambuya told her about other families who were in the same predicament. Knowing that one is not the first to be eaten by a crocodile does not make its teeth less sharp or its breath sweeter.

But Ambuya repeated the same story whether they were shelling nuts, weaving baobab mats or just sitting in the shade in the afternoon sun. "Your grandfather was a rich, fearless, brave man. When the kneeless came, he was the only one who stood his ground in front of his cattle, defending them with his spear, axe and dog. Never forget that. He was a real man worth the member between his legs."

That explained why, whenever Chinongwa imagined her grandfather chasing vasinamabvi after they had beheaded him, she saw his member swinging down to his knees. She didn't feel the pride she was supposed to from having the blood of such a distinguished ancestor.

Many times while on the lookout for the baboons, walking to the well, coming back from fetching firewood or simply sitting behind the hut warming herself in the first rays of the sun, she would wonder, "How can I feel protected in this world if my own grandfather has no head? He can't see or hear. There is no use sending prayers to him. I can only be given away. What can one expect from a headless protector?"

The only person in whom Chinongwa had confidence was one of her mother's brothers, Sekuru Taguta, The Fat One. When Muraswa was given away, it was his season to work for mutero, the yearly head tax that every adult male native had to pay to vasinamabvi. Like many other clans, the Taguta males took turns to work for the one-pound-per-male-per-season tax. When Sekuru Taguta came back and found out that the fruit of his own sister's womb had been given away to an old man, he was devastated. "Where I come from, we don't give daughters away. I don't care how many girls were given away in your husband's family; your daughters are an extension of me. I am going to give the promised his cattle and millet. Muraswa will not be given to an old man as long as I have life in me."

It was when he approached Muraswa's betrothed that the latter hastened to collect his wife-to-be, declaring, "What is given is as good as eaten. Now she is mine, I would rather my vahosi look after her. Where were you when her parents needed food? Was it you or me who saved the Marehwa family from starvation?"

His earlier promises and reassurances that he would never dream of taking Muraswa from the breast of her mother vanished. So, just as Ambuya had always said, "Muraswa, with milk on her nose, became a wife."

After this episode, Chinongwa breathed anew, reasoning that Sekuru Taguta would be there for her. And he was. The last three seasons he had allowed her father and brothers to work for him during the dry period. That meant the men were able to work in their own field during the rain season. Even then, all concerned knew that it was done to save face. They never worked enough to repay all the millet he gave them. It was just a way to keep his sister afloat. His wife, who possessed a snake's tongue, made sure the Marehwa family understood that she thought of them as hand-peckers.

9

2

One morning while Chinongwa was sweeping the yard at sunrise, she heard the drum announcing a man's death. She went on with her work while faces of possible candidates filed past in her head. When her mother's piercing wail struck her ears, she dropped her broom and scrambled to the hut, only to see her mother bolting towards the main village.

For a while among all the howling and general disorder, she could not make out who the deceased was, but she felt so excited that she could hardly breathe. She turned towards Ambuya's hut, and saw her grandmother rolling herself in the dust in front of the entrance. Chinongwa did not interrupt, but stood with her hands folded across her chest, listening.

"It's my fat one that Musiki has chosen; it's the fat one because he's the good one; he has a big heart and is generous. But tell me, what's going to happen to the product of his loins or the products of his sister's womb? And me? What you are waiting for, Musiki? Tell me, when will you claim me? Am I such a bad person you do not want me with you? I can no longer see, feed myself, or wash myself, and soon I'll begin shitting on myself, then I'll be at the mercy of that snake-tongued wife of his."

Hearing these words, Chinongwa's mounting fear exploded. It was Sekuru Taguta, The Fat One! The pillar of her protection had crashed at her feet, leaving her exposed, shivering. Like a wet hen, she silently walked back to her hut amid all the commotion. Seeing her shaking on that warm day, her aunts thought she was possessed by bad spirits and hurried to get a muzumbani bush. They rubbed her body with its crushed leaves while she tried to explain. "It's the noise, the crashing noise."

"Was it like thunder crashing?"

"No."

"What then?"

She realised that nobody else had heard. The harder she tried to explain, the more furiously the women rubbed her—until she gave up.

It was much later, just before sunset, that she was able to drag herself to Sekuru Taguta's compound. When she looked at his lifeless, swollen face, she felt anger rising in her little chest. Even he, in whom she had put all her trust, had let her down. She had no tears for him. She quickly left the hut and went outside to listen to the singing, which was much more soothing than looking at her uncle's now useless body. While she sat and listened to the pounding drums and the singing, watching the villagers hopping up and down in unison, she felt her anger subside, but still she could not explain the sudden reflex she had had to slap her dead uncle's face.

The next day, after the burial and the deceased's belongings had been dispersed amongst his clan, Chinongwa heard her family's name called among those of the other debtors. Someone had been accounting. His wife. That meant the door to her granaries would be closed to them. Chinongwa knew the widow despised her family so much that she would rather ask complete strangers to work for her than her father.

That their land was less than half the size of what Sekuru Taguta had possessed, and consisted mainly of rocky terraces claimed from the hill, was lost on the new widow. She had never approved of her husband feeding his sister and her good-for-nothing husband. Although she had cried when Muraswa was taken, she took great delight at the sight of her full granary and the power it gave her.

***

A week later, Chinongwa was plaiting Ambuya's grey hair while the old woman soothed her. "It's not as if your parents are lazy. They just do not have enough land to feed the whole family. All because of your stupid grandfather. Instead of wanting to fight, he should have just run away with his cattle. He would have arrived at the settlement earlier and chosen fertile land. The vasinambvi never crossed the Mucheke River."

Chinongwa kept her hands moving deftly, knotting the hair here and there, only half listening. Her tongue was out and she was concentrating on her task. She had heard this tale before, though each time it varied slightly.

Chinongwa knew that her paternal grandmother had reached the settlement long after everybody else because she was waiting for her husband. When, finally, she did arrive, all the fertile land had been taken. To eat, she gave away her two daughters. Two seasons later, plagued with remorse, she lost her reason and spent her days complaining to her long-beheaded husband about vasinamabvi, whom she saw and heard wherever she went.

Examining Ambuya's blind eyes, Chinongwa wondered why they were able to cry but not see. What she wanted to ask was why the old lady sometimes called her dead paternal grandfather stupid, and sometimes said he was the bravest of men. But she held her tongue.

She did not know what to believe. She knew that many men went to work for the colonisers who in exchange gave them food or sometimes money. Most stayed just long enough to earn enough for mutero for the season. But some never came back and nobody knew what happened to them. There was a rumour that vasinamabvi were kidnapping and then forcing them to build an iron road that led to their woman king, while another insisted that those who did not return had been sacrificed to the gods of vasinamabvi. What Chinongwa could not understand was why they ever went in the first place, especially since her father had never gone.

Chinongwa's father had never worked for the colonists because his younger brother did so every now and then and gave him the pound for mutero. What Chinongwa did not know was that her father was terrified of vasinamabvi. Ever since he had witnessed them killing his father and taking his head with them, he could not forget how he had shat on himself. At the mention of the kneeless, he could still smell his own shit. His worst and most secret fear was that one day his recurring bad dream might become reality.

In the nightmare, he's sitting with the village elders at the dare and there's a smell that only he can identify. He dares not stand up. He always wakes up when the headman orders every man to do so, one at a time. Would he one day be caught out?

Three moons after the death of Sekuru Taguta, The Fat One, Chinongwa and her mother took Ambuya to give her a mourning cleansing at the river. While Chinongwa scrubbed her back, Ambuya prattled on, "Vasinamabvi must have brought their tainted winds and thrown them at us. Unheard of crimes are being committed. People are planting axes into the heads of their neighbours, all for land. Brother is burning brother's hut with the whole family inside, all for land. And when one brother dies, all the other

14

brothers and paternal cousins fight to inherit his widow, not for her fat thighs as it once was before the removals, but for that piece of unfertile land that she now possesses."

Chinongwa's mother did not want her mother to talk about adult affairs in front of Chinongwa so she admonished her mother, "We're not alone; the child is present."

But Chinongwa was relieved to be trusted. She was not very concerned about who was going to inherit Sekuru Taguta's wife, or his land. Far more important was what was going to happen to her? From what Ambuya had said, she understood that for her family to survive, now more than ever, her fate was sealed. She could not forgive Sekuru Taguta for dying when he did.

***

One day during the following dry season, Chinongwa was sitting in the shade and chatting with her grandmother who was shelling peanuts while her grand-daughter scratched her back. Though she did not believe everything Ambuya said, she enjoyed listening to her; what she valued most about the old lady was that she was the only one who gave her answers. She could ask the same question three times and Ambuya would never remember that she had responded to the question before. Sometimes her answers varied, and in this way, Chinongwa was able to guess the progress of her destiny.

Chinongwa complained that her mother and father preferred her brothers. "And my brothers do not like me either. They never play with me, or bring me the seeds from the flamingo trees for making beads—not like other brothers do. Fourth brother Tafadzwa brought me some just once, but he's the only one to have done so."

"Ah mwanasikana, they like you, they do. All brothers like their sisters."

When the peanut shell was hard to crack with her now weak fingers, Ambuya used her teeth.

Rubbing yellow mucus from her sore eyes, Chinongwa pressed on, "Then why do they not talk to me or play with me?"

"All four of them are much older than you. They have their own lives, their men's world that does not include women. I'm sure they have some brotherly affection for you, like you have a sisterly one for them."

Chinongwa was not sure she possessed such sisterly affection, so did not answer.

"But don't forget, they feel guilty because you're going to be given away so their stomachs can be filled. Even though they will never be traded for food, thanks to that member hanging between their legs, they're not proud to be saved by a little girl like you. Without you, they're nothing. You're bigger than yourself, larger than the four of them combined, and they know it. Now that Sekuru Taguta, The Fat One has left, you know what your father is going to do, don't you?"

Chinongwa nodded. Suddenly weary, she dropped the scratch-stick down Ambuya's back. "Everyone hates me!" she said bluntly.

The old woman removed the stick and pulled Chinongwa towards her, holding both her hands tightly. "It's not easy for any-body, mwanasikana. Though exchanging daughters for food is an age-old custom, those who do it are accused of giving their village or tribe a bad name. And those who exchange food for women bring respect to their villages. Your family has offended the village. Your brothers are suffering too."

Chinongwa burst into tears and the old woman began stroking her and trying to wipe her tears away. "What did I do to be so hated?"

"Chinyarara mwanasikana. Ngoni and Tichafa have also been laying their marital traps without any visible results. Their hut-brothers are married. Some of Ngoni's hut-brothers are on their second wives."

Chinongwa sniffed and wiped her eyes. "But that's because Tete Shorai is not looking hard. Mukoma Ngoni says so. Two whole seasons and she has not found anybody. Do you think she is looking hard? At the last rain dance, many girls danced with Ngoni. If they did not like him, they wouldn't have danced with him. That is what Mukoma Ngoni says."

"My dear child, many of these girls are well brought up. They are taught to respect everyone. I'm sure your aunt is doing her best, but there are some families whom she cannot even approach. She does not want to be told to her face that no one wants to marry her nephews. What Ngoni needs to do is go to another village far away, a few days walk, where nobody knows him."

"But how will he know where to go? And if nobody knows him, they will not marry him. Or will he go with Tete Shorai?"

"No, mwanasikana. He'll go to a village where there is a cousin or uncle, stay long enough to be introduced, then when he finds himself a bride, either he stays in the family for five seasons working for his bride or he stays two and your father sends two head of cattle. When I first suggested it, Ngoni wouldn't hear of it, but now I think he agrees with me. He has understood that his chances here are small, he has. Have you noticed his talk of having two wives has also disappeared? Maidens are not fruit that anyone can pick off the ground. Ngoni should be sent away to hunt for a bride, otherwise he will die a tsvimborume."

"What is a tsvimborume?"

"A man who never marries. When he dies, a mouse is tied onto his back and he's told that it's his child. That way, he does not come back to haunt his family looking for his children. Because he can't see what is on his back, he thinks it is a child."

"What do you call a woman who is not married?"

"All women are married!"

That night Chinongwa dreamt of herself as a tsvimborume, with the village elders determined to tie a mouse onto her back. They knew she was a girl, and she kept telling them she was not dead, and yet they persisted.

As days and moons passed, Chinongwa's senses grew sharper as she tried to determine her fate. Just before the rains, Ambuya called Chinongwa to help her bathe. Chinongwa brought her the water that had been sitting in the sun and was as warm as if it had been on the fire. Ambuya did not like cold water. Pulling her along by her walking stick, Chinongwa brought her behind the compound and made her sit on the washing rock. Though she did not enjoy washing her grandmother, she could stare at her naked body to her heart's content. Most of all, she was intrigued by her grandmother's wrinkled breasts, which reached down to her waist. She used to touch them 'accidentally' and then watch them wobble. After scrubbing her all over, she would splash water over her back with a gourd and watch it seep into the soil at her feet. Ambuya enjoyed this the most and shrieked like a small child. When the water was finished and her head was dry, Chinongwa rubbed oil into her greying hair.

While she washed her, she asked questions, trying to discover if she had been the subject of conversation lately—or if they had found a groom for her. Ambuya, believing that Chinongwa was the only grandchild who cared for her, comforted her by trying to convince her that being given away was not the worst that could happen to a woman. Today, feeling that Chinongwa was more worried than usual, she tried to tell her that maybe she was not going to be given away after all.

"I hear your Tete Shorai is going to give your parents more millet. That should be enough to take you to the sowing period and, once there, who knows? We could go on like that until you reach marriageable age. When I could still see, I used to give your mother millet, but now I depend on the wife of The Fat One. Once she gets inherited, I do not think she will want to look after me. Already I know she eats better food than she gives me. I only get one piece of meat while she fills her plate. Her children tell me so. I hope she gets inherited by a man who will put her in her place. Taguta, The Fat One, let her grow a tail."

Chinongwa did not care about widows with or without tails and could sense that her grandmother was just trying to comfort her.

***

So much time passed without a word of a husband that Chinongwa decided the crisis was past. Life went back to normal and, little by little, her anxieties eased, though she was torn between not minding those chores that she disliked most and feeling guilty for any mishaps that she felt she had caused. For instance, she had always hated keeping a look-out for monkeys and baboons. The latter scared her and the former nearly always managed to sneak into the field whether or not she was attentive. But then she felt guilty for not preserving the little food they had growing and for not telling her family about the theft. At moments like these, she felt she deserved to be given away. As time went on, the pile of maize cobs, ears of millet, groundnuts and other crops that the monkeys and baboons made away with, loomed so high over her that she felt that nothing she could do would ever be enough to repay the lost food.

She knew not to tell anyone that she fell asleep on the watch, not even Ambuya. But while she slept, she was aware of where she was and that she should not be asleep. And the dream was invariably the same: father baboon ripping her apart or her own father catching her sleeping on the job. She felt relieved when harvest came and the whole family went to the fields with her to bring everything in.

The part of the harvest she liked best was when villagers went from family to family to thresh millet and bring it home. This usually lasted a month and felt like one long happy drunken spree. There was plenty of food and meat and by the end of the day most of the adults were drunk. Everybody ate to their heart's content and even the dogs were overfed. When she thought of it, she could not help picturing the singing, the dust, the flails rising, swinging over heads and then descending to pound to the rhythm of the music. The women would be ululating and swinging their bottoms provocatively while the men sang in thick, deep voices. She could feel the music in her body and wanted to dance, dance, dance until Musiki came for her.

The only thing she dreaded was the women of her mother's clan 'singing' her father for selling Muraswa. They said he was not a man, and he sang in reply that if only they could taste the manhood between his legs they would know otherwise.

3

It was after the third cock's crow that Chinongwa woke up. She thought she could feel warmth from a kindled fire and hear her mother's sniffing, but she wasn't sure. A fire suddenly flaring up on its own without her having to blow at it was suspicious, but she did not mind as its warmth caressed her body from the toes up. She loved the familiar smell of dry grass and semi-wet twigs burning, and the warm smoke filtering into the thatch grass.

She knew the cat had not finished the burnt sadza left-overs from last night. She felt that scarce sadza should be given to the dogs and not wasted on the cat, but her mother insisted otherwise. Only recently, Chinongwa had complained, "After all, the dogs hunt and help chase baboons away while your cat just lazes around the yard. There are rats and mice everywhere! Your cat just seems to look at them with a mixture of fear and suspicion while waiting for them to disappear before falling asleep again. But then who am I, a girl, to have an opinion?"

"One ceases being human once one can no longer look after an animal. One becomes animal oneself." Her mother responded as she swept the yard while Chinongwa drifted behind her, irritated by the answer she knew would come.

"But the other day there was a cobra inside the cooking hut while your cat was fast asleep beside the fire. Other cats would have sunk their claws into it before it could show its tongue."

Her mother had another ready answer, "It was no ordinary snake, child. Normal snakes are afraid of cats; this one had been sent. We owe so much to so many, it could be anybody telling us to not forget to pay back."

Even though her father had burnt the herbs inside the cooking hut, the episode stayed fresh and frightening in her mind, giving her the shudders. Many times since, she had fancied seeing the snake curled up here or there: she saw it curled on the path to the well or curled behind the bush where she passed water. At times, she was sure she felt it curled on her bedcovers while she slept and she would scream for her mother. In reality, the image would soon transform itself into a stone, a pat of cow dung or a large mushroom, but she still kept her eyes open; she was terrified of stepping on a snake.

Several times she saw the snake in her dreams, and the last dream she even recognised the owner, a woman she had always believed to be harmless. Presently Chinongwa saw the snake's mistress coming towards her. Though she was enveloped in mist, Chinongwa recognised her silhouette. "She must have maize-meal porridge in her bowl, my favourite. I can smell it. She has put some peanut butter in it. Oh no! I must not eat it. My mother will kill me. I am not to accept food from people, no matter how hungry I am. It could also be poisoned. Musiki help me! She's pulling me by the legs! She'll make me fall. Mai!"

As she kicked and pushed, she heard her mother's soothing

voice. "Chinongwa, Chinongwa, here, your favourite porridge. It is only I. Here, have some now. Quickly, before it gets cold."

Her mother was in the hut unusually early, a fire was already burning and she was offering her porridge. But her voice sounded strange. Chinongwa was not sure if she was still in the dream or not.

"Mother, I thought … I thought it was … But what are you doing here?" She could not bring herself to say she had mistaken her mother for the witch. But what was her mother doing in the cooking hut? She looked out; it was just another dark night. There was still moonlight; dawn was a few cock crows away.

The last time her mother had made the fire in the morning was when Chinongwa had nearly died. Was that not four rain seasons ago? Muraswa was still there. Mother, Ambuya and Tete Shorai had slept in the cooking hut. The neighbouring women had taken turns to come and night watch.

By the time Muraswa left, Chinongwa already knew how to make a fire, one of the first chores every girl was taught. Every woman passed through this obligatory rite; she woke up before everybody, lit the fire, heated the water for the men to splash their faces, and prepared the first meal of the day. That morning, her mother had already broken three rules: she had made the fire, she had made food for her daughter and she had woken her up gently. If one made the mistake of oversleeping, her mother usually just threw the covers off. And if one did not get up fast enough, she crowned it with a slap on whatever part of the body was handy. Now that she had entered her ninth year, Chinongwa rarely needed her mother to wake her.

Then, suddenly, like a bolt of lightning, it hit her. This was it. But who said she was ready? Wasn't she supposed to be warned? How come Ambuya had not said anything? This was not how she had imagined it. Yes, she had waited for and dreaded this day ever since she became aware of being alive, but was she not supposed to

23

see it coming? Was she not supposed to be the first one to know? Had she not kept her eyes and ears open all along?

Then the storm in her stomach started rising. The wind was blowing towards sunrise, towards sunset, to the north, to the south. She was choking. It had to come out or she was going to explode. Which way was it going to be? Up? Down? She had to get out, quickly before she wet herself or worse. But she had nothing on. She did not have a clue where her dress was, but there was no time to look for it. She had to act quickly or it was going to be too late.

Between her and the door was the fire. On the fire was a huge clay pot full of water, which was just about to boil. The fastest way for her to get outside was to jump over the fire. But when her mother saw her daughter jump, her instincts told her to hold her back. And her mouth started chanting, "No, no, no, no!"

Chinongwa felt herself being pulled back into the hut. As mother and daughter wrestled, either one of them, or both, kicked the clay pot, which overturned. All Chinongwa heard was a scream, which she then realised was coming from herself. The hot water was burning her legs.

Her mother was also screaming. The two could not see for, when the pot broke, some of the water ended up in the fire and all the ashes went up. They were both coughing and spluttering, trying to find the door with their hands, without opening their eyes. Luckily the mud floor had absorbed most of the water. Finally, they crawled out.

Baba Marehwa grabbed Chinongwa and pinned her to the floor. She did not resist. She was tired and her feet and legs felt as if they were still on fire. She was still crying. Not loud any more, but whimpering like a wounded dog. She tried to loosen herself from her father's grip. All the while, she did not stop murmuring, "My legs, my legs."

Her father ordered her to shut up immediately. "You're not going anywhere. I'm your father and I make the rules here. I'm not going to have my own flesh and blood defy me. I gave you the life in you, I decide what to do with it. What I say is to be obeyed."

Through her tears, Chinongwa could see her mother sitting with her legs stretched in front of her, her back against the wall. She was not making any audible sound but tears were flowing down her face and her lips were trembling. Though the only light came from the moon, the anguish in her face could be clearly seen. When Baba Marehwa saw his wife crying, Chinongwa felt his grip loosening. He wondered how he had managed to sink so low. The sniffling filled the night air and mixed with other night noises. The mocking laughter of the owls and hyenas could not have been far away.

Baba Marehwa silently lamented, "Laugh, hyenas, laugh! Were I you, I would be laughing too, but beware, were you me …"

Chinongwa suspected the witches had sent the hyenas and owls to snoop. Had everything been normal, she would never have sat down there while owls swooped around the hut. Even when she felt the owl sitting on the roof while she slept inside, as happened from time to time, she always felt suffocated. When Muraswa was still there, they would hold onto each other and relax only when they had heard it fly away. Sometimes, her father would come and burn some leaves and roots that sent the owls elsewhere.

Chinongwa's mother never cried. Of course, she had when her first daughter was taken away and at Sekuru Taguta's funeral, but that did not count. Her father must have been as touched by this as she was, for when he saw his wife crying, he went and sat down beside her, his head hung low. Chinongwa kept her place.

When Tete Shorai arrived, ghostlike, she said nothing but stared at the three silent figures. At first, Chinongwa decided that her aunt had been woken up by their screams, for her hut was close by; but when Chinongwa saw that her aunt, like her father, was fully dressed, she concluded that she was complicit in the plot.

Then she noticed her two older brothers standing behind Tete Shorai. She examined all the faces around her. Was it the night or the guilt on their faces that made them all look so ugly?

All these people standing around me, she thought, they do not care for me. They all want to get rid of me so they can fill their bellies. They just care for themselves. My brothers are happy that they are boys and will never be given away. They are loved, while Muraswa and I are regarded with contempt because we are girls. Tete Shorai, even though a girl, wants me to be given away anyway.

Chinongwa's bitterest anger was reserved for her aunt. She hates me, or she would be saying to my father, "You can't do that to my niece. I shall cut strings with you brother if you give my niece to strangers." I know that is how many aunts fight for their nieces. Their fathers are afraid to cut strings with their sisters so they let their daughters marry whomever they want. But Tete Shorai never defended Muraswa, and she will not defend me.

Then she thought about her mother. Does she dislike me as well? How could she let go of me like that? She even woke early to prepare me for my fate. Did she do the same for Muraswa? I'm shameful to everybody. Well, when I go, I'll never want to see them again.

She was not as angry with her father. Many times, her grandmother had explained to her why only women were given away. "Girls do not reproduce their own name. They bring forth offspring for strangers. They receive, carry and bring forth other people's seeds. Their own names, they sweep off the surface of the earth."

4

After the hot water incident, Chinongwa relaxed. Maybe Musiki had taken pity on her. How could it be explained otherwise? That it had happened on the very day they were to leave could only have been a sign from Musiki. Even a blind person would have seen it. And when she overheard Tete Shorai voicing the same doubts, she felt more like celebrating: maybe my beheaded grandfather has finally found his head, she thought. If, because of my burns, they are not going to give me away, then I am happy to have been burnt. Perhaps Sekuru Taguta, The Fat One, is already protecting me.

For a whole week, her father wavered from left to right and to the left again. He was not going to go against Musiki, but what was to be done? There was nothing to eat and the sorghum that Shorai had given them behind her husband's back was nearly finished. Their stomachs, which did not know what was happening and felt no pity for anyone, groaned with emptiness.

So two weeks after the incident, Baba and Mai Marehwa and Tete Shorai escaped for a little consultative walk even before Chinongwa woke up. She was throwing away the previous evening's ashes before rekindling the fire when she saw them coming back in single file. She stood, watching their approach, not knowing whether to greet them or not, whether to be angry or to simply ignore them. She could tell they had been to the n'anga about her. When the adults saw her, they stopped in their tracks as if they had been caught stealing.

Chinongwa's knees and hands started trembling. She let go of the clay pot which was full of ashes. She must have been holding it high because when it hit the ground it smashed and she found herself covered in grey dust and ashes. Her mother, who in normal circumstances would have screamed at her, just stared. Chinongwa took this as a bad sign. Then, for one fleeting moment, just enough to blink, her eyes locked on to her father's and she knew she had lost. The river was flowing against her. Or was it she who was swimming against the current? Whatever omens had been on her side on the day of the hot water had let go. She was all alone. She was shaking like one does in an early morning cold drizzle. Not violently but constantly. She went to pass water just behind the cooking hut because she felt she could not go very far. She did not care if the whole world saw her. With a twig she took some of the wet mud and plastered it on her burns and watched it fall down. She had been treating her burns that way.

She was still shaking and did not trust herself on her legs so she sat down just beside her water and with the twig started drawing pictures in its mud. Where the flow had ended, she could still see the white bubbles and could smell the mixture of urine and earth. It was a familiar and rather reassuring smell. She drew a few more circles in it.

Her legs were stretched out in front of her and she was inspecting the progress of the healing. Most of the burns were drying well and she was generally satisfied. There were three big ones that were taking their time, thus reminding her every day of her unfinished duty. One was just above her right knee and the second was above her right foot. The third, on her left arm, was the worst. It was proving to be stubborn. As some of the burns dried they left scabs that she picked off, something her mother had forbidden her to do.

"One should not skin oneself alive. If people see you they will suspect you are a muroyi."

She knew she should go back and light the fire and start the day, but she could not move. Something wet fell on her naked thigh. It was a tear. I wonder why tears are always warm, she thought. You would think they should be as cold as spring water.

Then she felt as if she had something stuck in her throat. She tried to swallow, but it would not budge and she gave up.

She looked up but did not see anything. The sun was just rising and its rays were in her eyes. It made strange and beautiful lines across her vision. Red and orange. She kept blinking. Even when she closed her eyes, she continued to see the lines. Then she had to stop the game because her tears had ceased. It was one of those annoying, stupid things; when one does not want to cry, tears flow without asking permission, and when they are given permission, they dry up.

She decided she was going to pass more than water so she went out of the yard and climbed the little hill behind the family compound. When she finished, she still did not feel like going home and decided to sit on her favourite rock to meditate. This rock was like her private cradle. She went to it when she was happy and felt like celebrating, and when she was sad and needed comforting. The rock never asked any questions; it understood her every mood. It was shaped like a well-used grinding stone and she always lay down in the place of the grain. The rock rose a bit behind her as well as to her left and right. This way, she was well protected from any intruders except if they came from right in front of her.

29

But she was most likely to see them first, for she was camouflaged by the branches and leaves.

From this height, the whole village was laid out in front of her. At this time of the morning, all the cooking huts were emitting smoke and resembled hillocks crowned in morning mist. On her left were her mother's people's settlement and, from this height, the round huts looked like grey mushrooms stuck to the ground.

Below her were her father's people's huts, which were slightly smaller in size than her mother's people's. Mostly, each family had one cooking hut, one sleeping hut for the parents, one for vakomana, another one for vasikana, then the elevated hozi for the millet. Those who had chickens had one even smaller hut on wooden stilts as high as a man in order to discourage the slender mongoose from pulling a chicken out through the woodwork at night.

On her right, out of sight from her mother's people's settlement, were Tete Shorai's husband's people. Because his people had arrived earliest at the settlement, they had the most fertile land, constantly fertilised by termites whose nests could be mistaken for unmoving elephants. Their huts were bigger and some of them had more than one hozi.

Chinongwa's parents' huts were built on the big granite rock used for threshing because there was not much land left when her paternal grandmother arrived. Unlike those of most of the villagers, whose walls were wooden poles dug into the ground and held together with bast and clay, her parents' huts had clay walls. They did not have a hut for girls so Chinongwa slept in the cooking hut.

Beyond the huts, to the east and all the way to the hills, rose patches of land divided by stone heaps that protected the soil from being swept downhill during heavy rains. Each family had its patches, which varied in size and fertility. Her parent's patches were the closest to the hill and therefore some of the driest and most infertile. But right now, everything was a rich green that would soon turn yellowish once the first vegetation finished eating the thin layer of humus last autumn had left behind. Chinongwa was staring at this hill without really seeing it.

Through the vegetation, rays of sun touched her body and made beautiful patterns, which kept moving up and down, to the right and to the left, according to the wind's instructions. The rock was singing lullabies to her. It understood why she was there. Peace was returning. A few birds were singing and from time to time human voices drifted up to her. They came from the direction of the main village, but she could not make out what they were saying. Not that she really wanted to know. In the past, when she and Muraswa played at putting words to the drifting voices, it was fun trying to guess what was being said.

"I understood that. The voice said, 'I shall come after the baby wakes up.' It was Mainini," Chinongwa would say.

"You deaf, withered grandmother," Muraswa responded. "'I'll come after the diarrhoea's dried up.' That's why her voice is strained. She's behind the bush, spraying it out, burning the leaves."

Both girls would burst out laughing and then stop to listen for more sounds to fit words to. A smile spread across Chinongwa's face as she remembered other incidents and what hilarious words Muraswa could dream up! How she always found something wittier to say. Presently, she could hear the voice of Ambuya floating back to her from last summer, "There are many girls vakabarirwa, and a lot of them find themselves sitting well. Better than they ever were in their own families. Better than some who marry for love."

"And what is kubarirwa?" Chinongwa asked.

"You're promised to your future husband even before you are born. The parents go to someone trustworthy and ask for provisions in exchange for the hand of the first daughter they will have. So when the girl comes of age, she's taken to her betrothed. In my cousin's village, there was a girl who was given to his father's

31

munyai. The man had three wives, but when the time came for him to claim his bride, the worthy man asked the girl to choose a husband from his three grown-up sons. Of course, the girl chose the best of the three. He was also the oldest one, and you know what? She became his vahosi, with two co-wives to rule over. She was happier than many a wife, and her husband was the envy of many who knew him. Nobody could tell that she had been 'born for.' So you see, she was happier than some who married for love."

Following that chain of thought, Chinongwa started dreaming of a similar scenario for herself. The man who takes me is not going to be old, she decided. He will be gentle and reasonable. A headman, perhaps. Someone respected by everybody. He will have many children and will be kind and wise. He will have uncountable cattle, sleek and fat. His milk hut will have zvirongo and zvirongo of milk. From the fresh for quenching one's thirst, to the thickest, ready to be eaten with sadza. His granaries will be overflowing with different kinds of millet, maize, rice and peanuts, and nobody will ever go hungry. He will give me to his first son. A clever man, like his father. I shall always have enough to eat and many people from far and wide will come and ask for food. My husband will come and ask advice from me. My brothers, now old but still hungry, will come to beg for food from me. Though I shall fill their bags, I shall remind them that they had given me away and that I would never forget this.

She left her rock and went down to the well, where she met Sarudzai, a girl of her age, who seemed surprised to see her. "How come you're still here? I thought they'd found a husband for you! Are these rumours false, then?"

Chinongwa threw a gourd of water at her and got a direct hit. Sarudzai was so surprised she did not recover until Chinongwa had balanced her chirongo on her head and disappeared round the bend. Chinongwa had even surprised herself. As she rounded the bend, half walking, half running, she felt elated. It was something she had always wanted to do but never believed she had the courage for. Sarudzai, like her mother, was a good gossip. Chinongwa despised her for that, but she hated herself even more for opening her heart to Sarudzai, fully knowing that she would spread everything she was told. And today Chinongwa was in an audacious mood. First, she had dared Mother to reprimand her for breaking the pot, then she had gone to hide so as not to be sent to watch the baboons, and now she had just splashed Sarudzai with water. She was jubilant.

"I hope they give you away to a blind cripple whose body is crawling with lice. He will whack you day and night, and …"

Chinongwa ignored Sarudzai's voice. She knew she had to keep going lest the girl decide to follow her. If she went far enough, Sarudzai would fall back, since her compound was in the opposite direction.

It is not easy to run away from an angry friend chasing you with the help of all the ngozi of her family while balancing a clay pot on your head. Not long ago, Sarudzai had made Chinongwa drop her chirongo. She had told Mai that she had dropped it when a snake had tried to bite her. Luckily, she'd dropped it near the puff-adder bend and Mother had not suspected anything. There was no way she would have told her mother it was because of Sarudzai. Discussing family matters with anyone was strictly forbidden, let alone with Sarudzai, the village gossip's daughter who, moreover, was showing promising signs of following in her mother's footsteps. If one wanted a message to spread like a bush fire, one whispered it in Sarudzai's mother's ear, not forgetting to point out that it was a secret. This made the gossip-monger grow wings, her heart would thump, and agitated, she would fly to the nearest person to relieve her chest before it burst. By the end of the day, the news would have spread throughout the village and beyond, and she would be breathing all the better for it.

Every bitter root serves a purpose. Though nearly everyone confessed to disliking this woman immensely, no one failed to see how useful she was. Through her, mothers-in-law sent messages to their daughters-in-law and daughters-in-law sent messages back to their mothers and sisters-in-law. When one was the recipient of a bad message, one of course forgot that one had also used the gossip to convey bad tidings, and so one longed to slap her on the mouth.

On her way back from the well, Chinongwa wondered how Sarudzai had known that she was to be given away. Had someone from her family sent her to tell me or was Sarudzai just being her mean self? But it was only this morning that they went to consult. When did they see her to tell her what to tell me? Are they really going to give me to a blind man? All the way home, she counted the blind men she knew and decided they were all most unsuitable. But she understood the search for a husband was now inevitable.

So, when before dawn the following day Tete Shorai came to wake her up, Chinongwa did not cry for the mother she would be leaving behind. She went along in a daze, as if obeying an unseen force. Her mother, who was standing arms crossed in front of her sleeping hut, watched her last daughter leave, not knowing when she would see her again. But she was relieved it was Tete Shorai in charge, so that she and Chinongwa would not have to confront each other.

Chinongwa knew her mother was standing there, could feel her eyes penetrating her being, but she refused to look back. Tete Shorai and Baba Marehwa, who had armed themselves to the hilt for the coming battle, were disarmed by her docility.

Chinongwa's departure from the village was a silent whisper.

5

It was their second day on the journey. Chinongwa's eyes were aching as if possessed. She would have kept them shut if she could. That morning, they had started with the third cock's crow and hadn't stopped until their shadows were between their legs. Baba Marehwa was in front, using his walking stick to find the path whenever he had doubts. Though the moon was nearly full, at times the path was hidden under grass that was heavy with dew. Tete Shorai kept a respectable distance from her brother. Maybe she needed that distance between them; perhaps she just wanted to slow him down.

Chinongwa was wearing her mother's old red and green pleated skirt. This was tied by string just above her fruits and it flowed down to just above her ankles. The string did not hold very well, and every now and then she had to pull the skirt into place to avoid tripping on it. Though the skirt protected her burns from flies and prying eyes, which was why she was wearing it, the fabric caused her much discomfort, for it kept rubbing or sticking to her wounds.

They ate their meal of cold rice in dovi with smoked beef under the muchakata tree and drank from the village well. Though satisfactory enough, Chinongwa would have preferred a hot meal of sadza with fresh pumpkin leaves in peanut butter. There was food left in the basket for another meal, but she kept hoping that they were not going to need it, that they would find a hot meal for the night and, with it, a mat to sleep on.

Tete Shorai was just as tired. Chinongwa could tell from her stingy mood. Had she had a choice, Shorai would not have come, but Baba Marehwa had no other sister at hand.

It was also in her own interest that Chinongwa be given away. Shorai's husband was well regarded in the community and had more than ten head of cattle to his name. She was the only wife and though he had never expressed any desire to have more, Shorai felt it was better and safer not to tempt fate. Though she was the most suitable person to accompany her brother and niece, she was free to refuse. But the thought of her husband having designs on her niece was forever present in her mind. This, therefore, was a small sacrifice for her peace of mind once her niece had been found a man of her own.

As soon as they'd finished eating, Baba Marehwa announced, "Let me go and offer snuff and introduce myself to that family weeding in the field. Or maybe you, Shorai, should come with me, no?"

"Maybe I should stay behind just in case they prove hostile. I shall keep my eye on you. If you want me to join you with the …" she nodded towards Chinongwa, who was lying on the grass in the shade.

Chinongwa was more than happy to rest her aching feet. Even though they had stopped to eat and rest, her feet had not stopped aching. Her whole body was tired and, after walking all morning, she was ready to drop dead. Now that she had eaten, her body kept begging for rest. She took the shawl that she had on her back, folded it for a pillow and lay down to rest, forever if she could. Tete Shorai contented herself with leaning her wide back against a tree trunk, blowing her nose and taking snuff. From time to time, she glanced at her sleeping niece and then at the family in the field.

It did not take Chinongwa long to fall asleep. At first it was bliss itself. Her bones stopped aching and her tired body surrendered to the spirit of unconsciousness. Peace enveloped her. But the bliss did not last long; she could see them after her; they were too far away for her to identify, but she knew they were coming for her. She had to run, but they were getting closer. She turned to look back and could make out Ngoni, Tichafa, Tafadzwa and Dambudzo in the crowd. Even her own blood brothers were after her. She had to run faster, faster than ever before. She could hear the pounding of hundreds of feet. Feet, dust, bodies, sweat. The blind man from the village was in front. She decided to reason with them, "But I can't. He's old and he hits children with his walking stick. Give me to anybody but a blind man. I beg you." But they could not hear her. Their feet were making too much noise. Neither could they see her fear. Their pounding feet raised dust, which mingled with their bodies, turning them into one advancing mass. They were excited; the men jumping into the air, waving their fists at her. Now the blind man was shouting, "Didn't you know you were born for me. I have come to claim you. I have the right to claim that which is mine." But how could he? He can't offer even a goat for me! And to find out like this. I must cross the river before they catch up with me. If only I could get there before them, I shall then turn myself into a mermaid and laugh at them. I could then come back into the village whenever I felt like and choose a young man with a young and beautiful body to be my love slave until I get tired of him, kill him and go back for another. I shall be the one to make the rules! But her feet were getting heavier. They had caught her. She couldn't

37

see them but she could feel them all over. She couldn't move. She was shouting at them to let her alone. They would not, and she had to hit them. Tete Shorai was with them, and it was she who was holding her down.

"Stop, child, you have got them bad winds all over you again. Your father returns with people and they're not going to hear you talking in your sleep. What will they think of you? You will have closed the cave entrance before you enter it. You will die an old maid and have a mouse tied to your back. Here, sit up straight and cover your legs properly like a well-bred woman."

Tete Shorai pushed Chinongwa's head back and squeezed more of the cursed muzumbani juice into her eyes, which stung a bit. She wanted to scream at her aunt that she did not care who thought what. She was sure her aunt suspected her of being possessed, but would not bring herself to say it. She wiped off the mucus around her eyes.

Her father appeared in the distance and was accompanied by three other people. An elderly couple and a middle-aged man, probably their son. The elderly woman had her front teeth missing and the few that she still had looked like grains of maize that had been forgotten in her mouth, ready to fall out at any moment. Her face was decorated with the tattoos of her tribe. A big leaf on her forehead and a smaller one on each cheek. The wrinkles stretched from the eyes to the mouth, curving round the cheek tattoos. Though her cheeks had sunk in where her teeth used to be, she still looked imposing.

The son was the male living image of his mother though he still possessed most of his teeth, except for three missing at the front. His round belly made him look shorter than he really was. Though he looked middle-aged, he drooled and his tattered shirt was visibly wet. He stared at the visitors as innocently as a child.

The elderly man looked older than his wife and his face was decorated with tattoos and suffering. He looked as sorrowful as a widower who has just buried a long-time wife. His wrinkles were so pronounced, they made his eyes seem sunk in their sockets. He had a faraway look that told you there was nothing new to discover. He seemed to be patiently waiting for Musiki to call him.

They shook hands and Shorai passed the snuff among the elders. Baba Marehwa's voice was shaking with emotion as he introduced everybody, "Now who would have known that today Musiki would direct me to her with whom I herded goats? Were our mothers not of the same blood? Is she not my cousin? Now look at her and her husband! And a son who is a man! Was she not like this when we separated?" Here he showed that she was not above his knees.

The elderly woman added her memories, addressing herself directly to Shorai. "We played mahumbwe together and it was your brother who taught me how to swim, who saved me from a leopard when it found me showing him its little ones, which I thought were kittens. I look older, but he was born four summers before me and he knew the difference between kittens and leopard cubs. Luckily, he had a spear, which he threw at the leopard while we escaped. You, Shorai, you were still on the breast."

After the removals, these people did not keep in touch, and in most cases nobody knew what had happened to the others. Those who had left together tried to keep together and start afresh in whatever conditions they found themselves. From time to time, distorted news of a dear and nearly forgotten one filtered through and was shared hungrily throughout the clan or village. Since news travelled from mouth to mouth, it grew more and more distorted along the way, depending on the numerous stations it touched. People would rejoice and jump up and down and women would ululate at the news of a loved one's marriage, even if it was already one or more seasons old. In the case of a loved one's passing away, fresh tears would flow freely, and people would gather around and hug, howl and suffer together. Even passers-by would stop and share in the weeping.

As Baba Marehwa and his long-lost cousin exchanged news, they cried freely and, after a respectable pause, everybody wiped their faces, blew their noses with the backs of their hands and the old woman passed more snuff around. A moment elapsed in silence. The only noise was a little sniffing, disturbed by babblers quarrelling in the muchakata tree. After a few uncomfortable twisting movements, Baba Marehwa launched into the reason for his journey. The toothless woman punctuated his narration with nods and grunts while her son kept throwing his eyes at Chinongwa. He was the hyena and she was the goat; he was trying to judge whether or not she was worth his while, whether she could make a decent mouthful.

Chinongwa was praying for the ground to open so she could hide from his persecuting gaze.

Meanwhile, Baba Marehwa continued in a monotonous, subdued voice. "When there is no more need to light a fire every morning, is a man still a man? When hunger has come into the hut, when it has laid its eggs and made itself at home, what choice does a man have?"

Here he nodded towards his daughter without looking at her. He kept his eyes trained on his left palm, which held his snuff. Shorai kept digging the ground with the fresh muchakata stick that she had just brushed her teeth with. The old man, who had found a rock to sit on, kept looking from left to right, avoiding the eyes of his guests, as if he wished himself anywhere but there. He gave the impression of one who was about to leave.

Unlike his father, the son seemed impatient to participate. Once or twice the son opened his mouth without uttering a word. He was bubbling inside and seemed in danger of exploding without warning. Chinongwa kept watching him, fearing he was going to pounce on her like a cat on a rat. She did not want to be alone with him. But the more he looked at her, the faster his heart beat in anticipation, and the faster hers beat in retreat. Suddenly, the son grunted and stuttered at the same time. The adults started as if waking from a stupor. All eyes were on him. Shorai seemed surprised that he was there. Baba Marehwa stopped talking. His mother had a resigned look as if watching a storm about to break and knew only too well she could do nothing about it. The father, his shoulders sagging, looked at his son as if he could see through him. Before anything comprehensible could come out of the son's lips, the father suggested the two of them should go back to the field. But no, the son was to be heard, and hear him they did.

"I was just proposing that since I do not feel like passing my whole life a tsvimborume, I could have her and the case would be solved here and now." He straightened up and smiled, feeling pleased with himself for solving this difficult problem for everybody.

His father replied in a soothing voice, "Maybe you're right. But why don't you and I go back to the fields and let your mother discuss it with her cousin. It is a woman's affair and you and I are in the way."

There was pleading in the father's eyes. He was choosing his words with great care, hoping that his son would not go into one of his fighting moods when nobody could stop him anymore. One wrong word could trigger an afternoon of misery. He held his hand out to his son while forcing a smile. You could read the pain in his face and eyes. Unlike the old woman, who from time to time spoke of her suffering, the old man only complained inside himself and once in a very long while, when no one was around, tears of self-pity would flow freely down his wrinkled cheeks. Later, he would be ashamed even though nobody had been there to witness his pain.

Whenever there was a funeral, the old man seized the occasion to cry for himself and his misery which, as a respected elder, he was not supposed to do. When most of their peers could now sit back and watch the births of their grandchildren, then first teeth, first steps forward and all the pleasures of parenthood for the second time, this old couple watched their unstable tsvimborume. The bachelor son, ignoring what his father said, continued, "After all, everybody says, 'Get married, find a wife, make your own home!' Well, today Musiki has answered my prayers. Look at what he has sent us! Did we go and look for them? Our ancestors, who know that I am here and looking for a wife, have sent me this here in front of us. The pen is full of cattle. What are we waiting for? All we have to do now is carry the fruits home. You, my old one, what are you preserving the cattle for? I am your first born and deserved to be married first. And yet, you let all my younger brothers marry before me. Look, my hair is now grey and I still do not have a wife. I am going to be the head of this family when you are gone, but how will they respect me if I am childless?"

Nobody replied. What the father had tried to avoid was happening. The bachelor son felt inspired. He grew wings. Of their own free will, as they always did, words came forth, "What made them eat their food here by our well? Why did the old man come to speak to us? Answer me! The ancestors have brought this to us. To me!" He smiled, raised both hands, palms out, and pointed at Chinongwa.

Once more, there was no reply from his audience. Just a lot of fidgeting. His parents were, of course, afraid to argue with him; and Shorai and her brother pretended to be occupied with their snuff. Chinongwa could only stare. She was no longer afraid, but numb. The babblers in the muchakata tree kept up their chatter.

"A woman is never refused. Of course, she is a cow coming from grassless meadows. But feed her a little and you will see those cheeks filling out like a squirrel's. I say let's take her!"

He gave such a wide, satisfied smile one could see the tooth gaps in the back of his mouth. His eyes were bright and shining, his whole face was lit up in mouth-watering anticipation. He did not wipe the drool off but let it run down the front of his tattered shirt. The stone-like gloomy faces which stared at him did nothing to dampen his spirits.

With apprehension, the father advanced towards his son and once again stretched out his hand towards him. He looked at his wife and the wife looked at her son. With a smile, she indicated that he should follow his father. Still wearing his triumphant smile, the son obeyed. She had smiled! he no doubt thought. She was going to bring him back a wife tonight! He got up and followed his father, feeling elated. He had given an inspired speech and, at the same time, found a way to get everyone out of a terrible mess. Now, all he had to do was wait for his mother to bring the bride home. He could hardly contain his excitement.

Behind father and son, the mother was explaining to her long-lost cousin where she thought he could go, which doors he could knock on or where hospitality could be found. She did not explain anything about her son, neither did they ask.

As the toothless woman left, she started rehearsing what she was going to say to her bachelor son, and how she was going to say it. What she was looking for were soothing words, a magic balm. What if she got her son married? How would his wife ever cope? They could give him one of these hungry child-wives, like Chinongwa, that people were offering around, without caring what the husband looked like. The parents were only too pleased to get the daughters off their hands in exchange for food. But how could she ever do a thing like that to anyone?

Even when she forced herself to imagine him married, she saw miniatures of her son, mouths half open, chests wet from dribbling. This helped her to stick to her resolution that their son should never marry. She didn't mind looking after him to the end of her life. After that, he would be Musiki's responsibility.

A womb that had brought forth four and ten, of whom twelve were still walking, could not begrudge Musiki for including one sour fruit. It was only a pity it had happened to the oldest. Every new moon, her oldest son would stand outside and vent his anger to all and sundry for three or four nights in a row. The séance would usually begin around mealtime, and would gather speed, force and eloquence towards midnight, then slacken and lapse after the first or second cock's crow. With this unburdening, her son's heart would lighten and he would sleep like a baby until the next day, when the shadows turned to the east. A few days later, he would return to his normal life, the village having been informed of the arrival of a new moon.

While the old woman was planning what she was going to say to her son, Baba Marehwa, Shorai and Chinongwa were on their way to the next village. Neither adult blamed the son, both were relieved that he did not belong to them. Still, they felt slighted about what he had said about Chinongwa. They had never been made to feel more beggarly.

6

So far, Chinongwa had been rejected by all who had seen her, and Shorai was mulling over taking the risk of having Chinongwa as a co-wife rather than face more humiliating rejections. Out there, every rebuff of her niece hit her as hard as if it were of herself. Though she had always despised her niece— away from home and in unfriendly waters their blood ties proved closer than before. After all, they were both Marehwa women with the same name and totem, and therefore against the whole world. When prospective families made slighting remarks about her niece, a sense of shame and rage made Shorai want to twist their fat buttocks out of shape or simply murder them there and then. Only the day before, to the amazement of both Baba Marehwa and Chinongwa, Shorai had grabbed her niece and marched her away from the piercing, degrading eyes of an old woman who had told her that her niece was neither fat enough, tall enough, beautiful enough nor lively enough.

"If they knew who we were before the removals, they wouldn't be talking to us in this way. It is people like this, who were nothing then, that dare look down on us now. No manners. But don't fear, I would never leave you with cattle-ticks like these. I would rather bring you back with us!"

Chinongwa had no answer to this except surprise that her aunt defended her. Even Baba Marehwa followed his sister, forgetting to say goodbye to the hosts, who stared at them and wondered why complete strangers would just turn up and ask them to praise their bare bones.

So, for the first time, Shorai looked at her niece objectively, something she had never really done. Though she still believed the strangers had no right to judge the girl, how other people saw her brother's daughter was a revelation. This brought her to a rather comforting conclusion that if no one was interested in her niece, how could her husband be seduced by such rags and bones? For she was nothing but red eyes, tears and a runny nose.

"Maybe that's why my husband has never been interested in her," she thought. "It was not just because he is upright. Chinongwa is just not attractive to any man."

Shorai had always feared that her brother might one day offer his daughters to her husband behind her back. The fear had blinded her so she had never looked at her nieces objectively. After Muraswa was given away, Shorai had breathed a sigh of relief but transferred her attention to Chinongwa.

That her husband might be repulsed by her thin, scraggy niece had never occurred to her, because an almost paranoid anxiety had often taken hold of her and there were even occasions she got so carried away that she imagined herself dead and Chinongwa being given to her husband as compensation, taking over her husband, children, home and all. The worst thing about her situation was there was no one she could talk to and relieve her mind. She could not speak about her fear to her husband lest she gave him ideas, or to her family for the same reason. All she could do was look at her niece and quietly wish her dead—or out of her life. On her knees, she would beg the heavens to bring her a solution before she either went mad or got rid of her niece herself. When the heavens finally decided to bring her the solution she had prayed for, they obliged her to participate. She just hoped that once she had got rid of Chinongwa, she would at last be able to sleep.

This was the fifth day since they had left home and they had tried more than two tens and five families in the different villages they had visited. These had not been the poorest villages and the people had not been unkind. They had been given food and drink and mats to sleep on. They had been given warm water to wash themselves, and peanut oil for their skin and hair. The only thing that they had not been given was a future husband for Chinongwa, and cattle and millet to bring back to the starving family back home.

Baba Marehwa now knew his introductory speech by heart. He had spoken it so many times and received the same questions and sympathy, but one look at his daughter and heads had been politely shaken and directions given for the next family to approach. He could no longer stand the rejections, the pitiful sight of his daughter or the blatant but well-intentioned lies the villagers uttered to save face.

"Yes, we would like to help, but there is nothing more in the granary. These are the only oxen we have and they serve us as draught. We did not fare any better after vasinamabvi came. We also gave our daughters for food. Times have changed."

Sympathy, pity, kindness—they had met with mountains of it. If only they could take these back to feed the hungry family back home.

And the family did not stop looking towards the east at dawn, noon and dusk. For each of the last five days, the mealie-meal had been getting lower and the amount of sadza in each bowl was less with each meal. Mai Marehwa had long renounced serving her boys from the same dish because the oldest ended up eating more than the youngest. This works only in time of plenty, when there's enough left over for the dogs and the hungry traveller. She now had a bowl for each of them. She did not want to see fights between blood brothers.

The boys supplemented their diet by finding root bulbs and wild fruit while they looked after the cattle. They also trapped birds using urimbo, which they spread on the topmost branches of trees where swarms of red-billed quelea came to rest. But these days the guinea-fowl and franklin that used to eat all the grain were a rare sight. The smaller children had never even seen the birds, although their cries could still be heard in the distance.

Mai Marehwa mourned for her daughter alone and in silence. She was glad when night came because then she did not have to suffer the pitiful looks from those who knew, and the questions from those who did not. Here, at the end of the day, she could let her tears flow freely. Tears for Muraswa, whom she had seen only once since her elderly husband took her away, were mixed with the ones she was now shedding for Chinongwa.

She prayed for her, "My own grandmother, and your own mother, all you who have long gone back to Musiki, please direct my daughter to a good, understanding man, regardless of his age, a man who will allow her to visit her mother, unlike Muraswa's husband. Lead her in the path of luck, I beseech you."

Increasing the tension, Tete Shorai's husband came every morning to check if his wife had returned the night before. He knew very well she hadn't, but it gave him something to do. Even though he remained the example of politeness itself, he made sure it was understood that he had not paid roora to have his wife absent, especially during the weeding season. They were not going to spread their famine into his household as well.

48

After being assured that they had not returned and there was no news, he would then sit quietly without talking to anybody, sulking. He did not have to say anything. They just had to look at him and guilt invaded them, so they fought to avoid his eyes. When he felt he had made everyone thoroughly uncomfortable, he would take his hat, which he always put on the bench beside him, and take his slow leave.

7

On the sixth day, Baba Marehwa and Shorai agreed to turn back home. They both felt tired and humiliated. If the two adults had been alone, the journey would have taken them two days, but with Chinongwa in tow, and in the state she was in, it would take at least twice as long. But they couldn't drive Chinongwa any faster than she could walk and she was too big to carry. Where hope had carried them forward, now shame and disappointment added to their burden.

What brother and sister feared most, was their arrival at the village. Of all the events they had imagined, none had them returning without food and with Chinongwa.

"It's not as if we didn't try. We've spent a whole week in the jungle. Many would have turned back after a few days. Who would have tolerated all those humiliations? They can say what they want, but I think we did what we could. One can't go against Musiki," Baba Marehwa told the family hosting them that night.

Shorai had been longing to hear her brother pronounce these words. She hastened to reassure him, "No one will say anything. If anyone disagrees, they can take her with them and find her a husband, and we shall congratulate them. As for me, I shall never undertake another such embarrassing trip!"

The hosts were obliging and made all the suitable, encouraging noises.

Most of all, Baba Marehwa felt inadequate. Not only was he unable to feed his family like a man, but nobody, not one single person other than that drooling tsvimborume on the first day, had wanted his daughter.

Chinongwa felt relieved. Hope came back and her heart beat faster. She kept quiet under the covers behind the hostess and pretended to sleep.

"If her footsteps were not meant to dance in the sand of these hills and valleys, well it is not to be. Tomorrow we reverse the direction of the wind."

Chinongwa fought the urge to kick her feet in the air to celebrate. Even though there were some expressions whose meaning escaped her, she had understood the essential. They were going back home, back to Mother. This ordeal was over and she had won. Her father and aunt were finally, like her, tired.

Every time she had opened her mouth to speak over the past days, instead of her voice coming out, tears had. When asked why she was crying, she had one word only, "Nothing." More recently, she had given up responding altogether.

One outcome was that people now believed she was deaf and mute. And who was going to give their cows for a deaf mute? Who knew why she was thus? As it was, she was a misery to look at. Of course her father and his sister insisted that she could hear, but how could one be sure? What if she had ngozi? One does not set out with a normal child and end up a few days later with a deaf mute for no reason.

Over the previous three days, the rejections had been swift and pronounced. The usual physical examinations had disappeared. Instead there was advice, "Why don't you go back and consult? Maybe Musiki is trying to tell you something."

Whenever people addressed Chinongwa, Shorai had started rushing in to answer for her. "Oh, she is well, but her legs, poor child, must be tired. We've come a long way." And to Chinongwa, "We have, haven't we, my father's one?" Chinongwa knew that Shorai, who was more afraid of the tears than the deafness, was telling her not to answer. She felt relieved and at the same time amused to see her aunt so uneasy.

So, while listening to her father and aunt talk about her sudden deafness and about turning back, she wondered why she'd not thought about it before. If only I had become deaf from the beginning, she thought, I would never have had to go through this. Or I could have become blind. Next time, if they try again, I shall become blind—and then we'll see what they do!

Then her thoughts wandered back to her hill, waiting for her with blood-red nhengeni at this time of the season. Just before she'd left, she had gone to say goodbye to these trees and had shed a few tears, knowing that she might never see or eat their fruit again. But now she rejoiced in the thought of returning to them. It was her private orchard that nobody else knew about; one thing that Muraswa had bequeathed to her. The first thing she would do was pick some nhengeni and, with her treasure gathered in her skirt, lie down on her favourite rock and eat them. Only the reddest of them would she pick, nothing but the best for her. She wondered if the wasps had built their nest on the third tree as they had done over the last two summers. She would have to approach it with great care. The first summer she had found herself assailed by these stinging insects on all fronts. For three days she had gone around with one eye shut.

While she had been thinking about her orchard, she had lost track of the adult conversation. Now she heard her father saying, "And I shall be left with only one ox. A family with one ox. But what choice does a man have? In any case, one of the oxen has got on in age and it is time to change it anyway. I shall exchange it for some millet now, and after the harvest I shall buy a young ox to replace it. I know I shan't get much for it. Before the removals, we used to get ten matengu for a cow or an ox, but these days, if one manages to get five, one is lucky. But tell me, how long does the millet last? Will it last until the harvest? No! Then what? I don't know what we're going to become. Oh, I swear on my father's headless body, we shall see what we shall see. Chickens will soon be talking."

Shorai wished her brother would stop and started fidgeting on the reed mat. The hosts kept their eyes trained on the fire. They did not know what to say to their guest that would soothe him. But Baba Marehwa had not finished. "Is it me who brought vasinamabvi here? I don't know where they came from. If it's a punishment from Musiki because we sinned, then let him show us what our sins were and we shall appease him. Then he can take them, their woman king, and their sticks that kill back where they came from."

The silence could be heard. Nobody answered Baba Marehwa. Chinongwa, who was growing tired of listening to the conversation, was fighting sleep. The hostess and Shorai were sitting cross-legged on the reed mat side by side around the fire. Both women had old thin blankets thrown carelessly over their shoulders and backs. Their palms, from time to time, were stretched out to the fire and then brought back to rest on their laps. These were the only movements the women made. They did not speak, and from time to time their faces would be lifted from the fire to the speaker's face. Behind them, Chinongwa kept trying to understand.

When the silence faded, the men, sitting on curved wooden stools, facing the women from across the fire, resumed talking.

Their voices were low and hoarse, and rose and fell with emotion. Had it not been for the grave countenances on the faces, this, from the outside, could have been translated as a peaceful gathering of long-lost friends. The well-fed fire gave out rays of amber, which blended with the bright multi-coloured clothes and rags that adorned the hosts and guests. The night was not cold but everybody huddled close to the fire, dragging its warmth into their troubled souls.

When Baba Marehwa was about to start again, the host, who did not understand why some people had decided to stay and fight the kneeless instead of just running away, cut in. "You people were lucky. You were warned. We were not. They torched our houses while we slept. If someone had warned me that the invaders were coming, I would have offered them my own daughter as a reward then taken my cattle to run, day and night, day and night without stopping."

Baba Marehwa didn't agree. "We were not at war with them, were we? People don't go to war with those with whom they have never shared snuff. When they came and sent their messenger to tell us that their woman king had bought all the land from our king, we thought the latter had gone mad. Whoever heard of anyone buying land? From whom? At what price? Who owns it if not Musiki? If they wanted land for their animals, why did they not come to see the headman like everybody else? There was enough for them and for us. What was there to fight for? But what do we know? We moved, did we not? It's the colonisers who have the land now, is it not?"

Nodding his head, the host answered, "Yes, you moved." He was getting tired of this whingeing guest and was trying hard not to be rude.

But Baba Marehwa desperately wanted the host to understand that he was of good breeding. "You should have seen the cattle. They were real cattle, not the half-starved goats that we take for cattle now. They were tall and looked a grown man in the face. They had long horns and were the colour of red earth. I saw them with my own eyes when I had seen four and ten seasons.

The host did not seem convinced and Baba Marehwa thought he detected an "I-have-heard-this-before" attitude. He went on furiously, "And game, it was everywhere. No child ever cried for meat. Now they tell us we cannot hunt because the animals now belong to the woman king. They punish you by sending you to build their iron road if you kill an eland or a sable."

Chinongwa had heard most of these stories many times over. What she wanted to know was what the adults were now going to do with her once they got back home. Their past did not interest her. Though her eyes were heavy with sleep, she was afraid to miss the crucial news, so she kept listening.

"We knew they were going to be there the next day. The man who brought the news said that they would shoot any man who dared stand up to them. But did my father listen? He ran after the man with his axe. He was going to chop his head off, his head and the bad news that he carried with it. He told the poor man to tell those vasinamabvi that he would rather die with his cattle at his home and be buried beside his mother's grave. Whether the man had been sent by the kneeless or whether he was just being kind to warn us we never found out. We never knew who he was. The elders refused to share snuff with a messenger of bad tidings, but once he had left, they drove off their cattle. The whole village, except my father, of course."

"Who then would have buried him beside his mother's grave if the village had left? He was a fool." The host had lost his patience.

With a voice hoarse with emotion, Baba Marehwa replied, "He tried to persuade everybody to stay, arguing that if the vasinambvi came and found everybody there, they would be frightened and would give up, but nobody believed him. Of course, at first everybody was with him … until some cowards recounted how the kneeless treated those who resisted."

The host felt the sting of the word 'coward'. He was not going to let Baba Marehwa off so easily. After all, he was in his own home. "Why did he think he would be able to fight the invaders alone when they had put down many a chief and his people? Had you not heard what they did to the Ndebele impis? Was your father worth more than a Ndebele impi? If we had sat down to talk to vasinamabvi, we might all still be where we grew up. But some of us decided to fight that which was bigger than us, and now look what the result is. What did we gain? Who is the king now?"

Chinongwa's sleep disappeared and her ears stood out. The two women had their mouths open, not understanding what was going on any more. Shorai wanted her brother to give in to the host. After all, they were in his home. She turned to confess her feelings to the hostess, but because she did not want to offend her brother, she swallowed her words without uttering them. The hostess was shocked that her husband dared attack a guest who was already down. Just when Shorai looked away from her, she glanced across at her in order to apologise for her husband's behaviour; but then she looked away again, grateful that she had not betrayed her husband. Both women concentrated on the fire, anxiously waiting for the storm to abate.

But Baba Marehwa was frothing. "These are not people that one can talk to. I saw what they did to my father with my own eyes. I survived by hiding, but they took my younger brother because he started crying when he saw them cutting off my father's head. My brother will tell anyone what they did to him. They are not humans. My father was a man among men, but what chance does a man have against a smoking stick that kills from far? Even if they had not killed him for his cattle, he would have died anyway. He would have joined the rebellion. He was not going to be anybody's dog as long as he was alive. Can we call ourselves men? Are we not dogs?"

The host did not answer. Baba Marehwa, feeling encouraged, went on, "All of us who survived are cowards. Cockroaches, nothing but cockroaches. We are women. Whenever we see the kneeless coming, we are shitting before they look at us. We are shivering like reeds in the middle of a stream. They tell us to move here and there, and we move. They tell us to pay hut tax, and we pay. They tell us to build their houses, their iron road, their mines. We do not obey our parents as much. 'Sleep here, my dog. Now get up, dog. Now follow me, dog. Chase the baboons out of my field, dog.' Oh, you're a man!"

The host had had enough. "Yes, I am a man in my home and I am my own master. If you do not think I am a man, why did you come into my home? Why did you ask for my hospitality? When you came in, did I ask you if you were a man or a dog? If your father was such a brave man, why are you going around begging for something to eat?"

"Give me back my hunting axe," Baba Marehwa said, standing up. "I'm not going to be insulted. We are leaving. Shorai, wake the child up."

The hostess pleaded with him, down on her knees, begging forgiveness for her husband's behaviour. Seeing it was not working, she appealed to Shorai to reason with her brother. "You are a woman like me. You have sense. You are younger than me, but here I am on my knees, making myself smaller than you. Plead for me, please."

When Shorai did not intervene, the hostess used the ultimate argument. "I shall keep the child. If you adults want to go because of my crazy husband, I shall not be accused of having chased a child out of my home in the womb of the night."

The husband, though still angry with Baba Marehwa for accusing him of cowardice, was regretting his outburst. He joined his wife. "Yes, Baba Marehwa, you can leave, but I shall keep your sister and the child for the night. The women will spend the night in my home. I have nothing against them. I have nothing against you either. It must be the bad winds the people from the north are sending us. We're killing each other for a 'yes' or a 'no'. Is that normal?"

Baba Marehwa was relieved by the hand of reconciliation. He sat down again and passed snuff. "Yes, it is the wind of vasinamabvi. And now they want us to give prayers to their ancestors. How can their ancestors be mine? If you start praying to the other's ancestor, who is praying to yours? I say those who are praying to the ancestors of the kneeless are lost forever. I admit we do not know where we are going any more, but at least we should know where we have come from. We should not forget to send prayers to those who came before us."

The hosts, pulling loudly at the snuff, agreed with everything Baba Marehwa said.

"If we start praying to the ancestors with those who are killing us, who will protect us?" he continued. "When your father dies, you bury him, and after the next harvest you go to his grave and ask his spirit to return to the family to protect you from your enemies and bad spirits. But if the invader has cut his head off and taken it with them, how can you bring him back? Even if he does return, how can he protect you without his head? What with their magic, our fathers might now be protecting them, not us. Who knows?"

The women, relieved, drew the men towards the weather—and other insignificant matters. The men did not need encouragement and, in no time, all were pretending the ugly exchange had never taken place.

8

The next day, they were up with the third cock's crow. Chinongwa was dragged off her mat and, in single file, the three Marehwas left the village. After seeing them go, their hosts could follow their guests' path with the help of the village dogs, which barked in annoyance as they passed. It was still dark and, though it was the middle of summer, it felt a bit chilly. Chinongwa kept close to her father and every now and then turned to see if her aunt was still behind them. Chinongwa was looking out for ghosts or witches; she kept worrying about how they could possibly defend themselves if they were attacked. Her father carried nothing but a small hunting axe that he hung carelessly over his left shoulder. That just won't do, she thought.

She remembered what Sarudzai had once told her, "You can't fight ghosts. You can't even see them. The most you can do is hear them moving around, or sense their presence. Even when they're riding you, you won't notice because you're busy sleeping." This made Chinongwa wonder if the witches were riding them all, sleeping or not. She looked at her father and wondered if the witches were riding him. She decided against it, because he was walking very straight.

While Chinongwa was worrying about all this, Baba Marehwa was worrying about her deafness. Has she really gone deaf and mute? He wondered. Until I've consulted a n'anga about where I stand, how am I supposed to know what to do? My eyes are no better than those of a blind man's. The first time I was about to set off, we were delayed by a pot of boiling water, but this time I consulted the n'anga before setting off.

"When you went onto the chikuva to tell your departed that you were taking your daughter for a walk, did you name your paternal great-grandmother?" the n'anga asked.

Baba Marehwa stammered. He did not really remember. The n'anga continued, "She felt jealous because you named your maternal great-grandmother. In her fury, she upset the hot water to frustrate your project. Go home, take her a gourd of cool water that you draw from the well before the village women get there. Tell her you recognise your fault and you regret it. Then water her. Wait two nights before you leave."

He had obeyed. If the voyage was going to be a failure, why was he not told? This time he would go to a different n'anga. Shorai's husband had told him he had once been to one who had greeted him by name and totem even before he had entered the consulting hut. Even if it was a two-day walk, he would not flinch.

Meanwhile, Shorai was wondering if the day she had dreaded had not finally arrived. She was the only one of the three girls who had not paid the family debt. There had been no justice for her two older sisters. It was normal that she should pay for this. She decided that her only option was to accept her fate. A husband such as hers—who was not old enough to be her father; who had always respected her; who had never reproached her, her family or

62

roots—such a husband could not come for free. She would have to pay for her privileges.

Of course, Shorai knew that she was considered by all to be beautiful. Her skin was as soft as a baby's, even in winter, and her eyes shone in the dark. Her breasts stood up straight and firm and she was tall and round. Her calves were full and her ankles and thighs were well padded. Her buttocks shivered when she moved. She had a beautiful smile and possessed all her teeth, which were as white as milk. Physically, she possessed everything a man could ever want. During droughts or famine, she could be counted on not to dry up and shrivel like a pumpkin that was picked before its time.

She was a full-bred woman who emitted confidence, a woman who planted roots solidly and deeply into the earth. She would not be blown by the first wind that came. She was a woman, a mother, a wife; she was a cave to hide in during storms, a well that quenched thirst during drought, a home to return to, a cradle to rock children to sleep; she was a passage through which life appeared, she was connected to eternity. Yes, she would train Chinongwa to love her children as if they were her own; she would teach her to love and respect their husband, and both would live peacefully with their children.

I am being punished because I never appreciated my luck, she told herself. Maybe if I'd been kinder to my two nieces who never wronged me. If I'd not felt ashamed of my two poor sisters, who were given away. If I'd not pretended, all these seasons, that none of my sisters were given away and that they did not exist. "If only I had been kinder to them when they came home for mother's funeral!"

She realised she had spoken out loud when Chinongwa turned to look at her. She stared back at her with piercing eyes and Chinongwa understood that whatever she had heard was not meant for her. She walked faster as an apology to Shorai.

The aunt went back to flagellating herself. Chinongwa has never wronged me, she thought, yet I've always disliked her and wanted her out of my life. If I treat her well, the two of us could perhaps become friends and look after our husband in peace and harmony.

With all these anxieties and regrets turning over in her head, Shorai's heart softened towards the miserable little creature trudging in front of her. Her being suddenly flooded with emotion. Had they been somewhere suitable, she would have held her niece against her and asked for forgiveness. As it was, she wept tears as she felt love for her husband and niece and guilt for her past behaviour; but they were also tears of self-pity, helplessness, surrender to fate.

The six feet plodded on in the semi-darkness, in silence.

Occasionally, the three surprised a kudu, a sable or an impala feeding on the morning grass, but a thousand hidden eyes observed them as the light grew: the man at the front, a hunting axe on his left shoulder, his trousers soaked with dew; the girl, holding up the front of her makeshift skirt to shield it from the dew; and at the rear, a proud woman balancing a basket of provisions on her head, as she walked with a straight back and sure, proud steps.

After leaving the forest and crossing the valley, the three stopped at a stream and ate the mapodzi their last hostess had prepared for them. If the adults had been alone, they would not have stopped until they had crossed the Mucheke River. Even though Chinongwa had not uttered a word of protest, her slow pace and her tears had been enough to make them pause.

After the meal, while Baba Marehwa and Shorai took their snuff, Chinongwa ran off to look for ripe hute. She picked from bushes growing in the shade, feeling the first return of a sensation that she had experienced only once before when her sister had been given away. She even giggled when she fell trying to follow a butterfly, or when she found a riper, blacker, juicier bunch of fruit, she smiled and dived for it. She did not name this feeling to herself, but it could be described as a return to childhood. She darted back and forth from the bushes, bringing the adults more and more hute.

The two adults barely noticed the abundance of fruit around them, while Chinongwa gathered it. Although surrounded by the music of the birds, cicadas, bees, frogs, wind and gurgling water, they did not seem to hear it. Even the song of the wood pigeon in the tree above them fell on deaf ears. Instead, Shorai saw her brother's face doing battle with its internal storm, beads of sweat running down his neck; she waited impatiently and without flinching for him to speak. Finally, while drawing more than the usual quantity of snuff into his nostrils, he said, "I suppose, Tete, we were born to it."

He did not have to call her tete. She was, after all, only his sister, and a younger one at that. It was the first time he had ever addressed her thus, and even though she was determined not to make what he was going to say any easier, her heart softened; nonetheless, she knew that he was addressing her as tete only because he needed her help.

"We're here to fulfil the roles that have been set down for us. Our footsteps are following the paths drawn for them. At times we try to wriggle out of it, but who are we to decide who does what and who goes where? Whose hand feeds whom? I'm not making this decision out of choice. I'm sure you know that my hands are tied behind my back. I am stuck against a rock, and it's you and only you who will be able to liberate me. I have tried to get out of this and I can't. I hereby put my fate in your hands. It is you who will now decide where we shall go and which path we shall follow. My path ends here, and I cannot move any further."

Shorai kept her mouth shut though she was bursting with emotion. What she wanted to do was pound someone—anyone.

65

But of course it wasn't done, so she fought to contain herself. Avoiding his eyes, she stared hard into the distance.

"You know what I'm asking you, my sister? Maybe it's for the best. We shall be keeping it in the family. I'm not insinuating that my m'kuwasha had other ideas. What would I know about that? Besides, it is you who would know his intentions. But one never knows."

Shorai had lost the game, but she would retain her dignity.

Aware that his words were like a razor cutting into his sister's flesh, Baba Marehwa reduced his voice to a whisper in order to soften the meaning. "Of course, you're free to say no if you do not agree with me. Only sometimes it is not prudent to refuse one's own flesh and blood. Your blood will never compare with a complete stranger's. Mind you, I'm not saying that your husband should have a second wife. There are many men who are content with one wife. Look at me."

But still Shorai said nothing.

"His father has three wives and two of his brothers already have two wives each. You will remind me that his oldest brother has only one wife, but no other woman would knowingly come and live with that snake. It is well known that she gave him a love potion. Regardless of her flat chest and dry buttocks, he has eyes only for her. Even if I were a desperate woman, I would never sacrifice myself for that woman of a man. One wonders where the children came from."

Here, both brother and sister had to smile. Shorai's oldest brother-in-law was a village joke. The other men always found strength in outshining this 'woman of a man'.

The moment was cut short by the appearance of Chinongwa. They both stared at her without speaking. They had forgotten her presence. It was Shorai who recovered first. All the anger she had been bottling up suddenly found escape:

"Well, and what are you staring at? Is that how you respect adults, by towering over them? Is that what I teach you? Wherever you end up, it will be me that they'll blame for not having done my duty by you. But if nobody listens to me, is it my fault? Your mother does not tower over people; I do not tower over people. The Marehwa are poor, but they're well-bred. Don't you destroy our name. If you come to live with me, you will have to mend your manners or we shall have many fights, you and I. And take those hute off your skirt before they bleed all over it!"

Shorai's earlier resolution from that morning to start to treat her niece with a softer hand had already been forgotten.

Slowly, Chinongwa walked away and let drop the fruit from her skirt. Though she had kept her pact and not said a word, her tears began flowing. She walked away until she was out of earshot, found a shady tree and sat down under it, her back against the trunk. Her tears fell on her skirt, so she moved her head a little to the left so they would fall onto the earth. This way, using a little twig, she was able to mix them with the damp earth. As she was not always successful in adding her tears to the mixture, the earth did not get as muddy as she had hoped. Slowly, she became distracted, now she wanted to cry, but her tears seemed to resist her. She bent her head lower to make sure not a tear was wasted. But as they dried, she began taking an interest in what was around her: the bees and the sunbirds, which hung suspended in the air, and darted from flower to flower.

For a while, her eyes and mind did nothing but follow them, but after a while her mind plunged down towards her aunt's words. Though she had not understood everything, she felt their weight. She did not mind the idea of marrying her aunt's husband. She quite liked him. But she dreaded going to live with Tete Shorai. She would rather live with a complete stranger. At least then the battleground would be level and one would be able to use what weapons one could find. But she was not going to do battle with her aunt. Even before the game had begun, she had lost. She could already hear her aunt's voice, "Thank me. I gave you my husband. Thank me. I looked after and fed you when you were starving." and, "You don't do this to my husband and you don't do that to my husband." He'd never be her husband: he'd always be her aunt's. She swore to herself that she would never be Shorai's co-wife. When we get home, she decided, I shall tell mother that I would rather starve to death. Those who are afraid of hunger can go and marry Shorai's husband. If they force me to, I shall run away. Only my mother shall I come back to see.

Though she had no destination in mind, the idea of running away itself seemed to be a solution. Somewhere in the world, there would be a place where girls who were forced to marry the husbands of their father's sisters would be able to find refuge and peace.

9

Had a storm not come and swept them into the nearest village, they would have continued walking until well after dark.

By then they were nearly running, but this pace seemed normal in the circumstances: who could afford to walk slowly when the mind was racing at such speeds? The mud-coloured clouds could not have been more fitting to their mood. So when the hailstones began falling, hitting them hard, they were not surprised. Thatch was being blown off the roofs and flew across the valley, to be stuck in trees. Hailstones pounded those cowering inside their roofless huts. Animals ran from bush to rock, looking for shelter; the smaller ones hit by the hail, were knocked unconscious or sent off to meet Musiki.

The three Marehwas ran to the nearest huts. As luck would have it, they were not very far away. Although in normal circumstances it is rude to walk into someone's hut without first clapping one's hands in greeting, the hosts were not surprised to see their number had suddenly increased. Even had the visitors announced themselves, they would not have been heard through the din that Musiki was making to show his power or his wrath.

At times like this, many had found themselves playing host to the most unlikely and sometimes unwelcome of guests—ranging from a frightened hare to a lumbering python. Of course, with snakes, matters were more complicated; but in the case of the hare, all one had to do was cover it with a big basket and prepare it for dinner the next day—without forgetting to thank those in the heavens who had directed it to the cooking pot.

Because of the smoke from the fire and the darkness of the storm, the hosts and guests could barely discern each other. But as their eyes adjusted, an adult woman, identifying Baba Marehwa as a man because of his voice, indicated a bench on which he could sit. She produced goatskins from behind the door and laid them down for Shorai and Chinongwa. All the while, she kept muttering excuses for their being wet, as if the sudden storm was of her doing, "I assure you it does not always start like this, I mean without giving warning. The clouds did not look as if they were carrying any rain until the wind got up, and then one did not have time to cough. It did not give you any warning, did it?"

"No, it did not," Shorai lied without thinking.

"Me neither … So I did not even have time to get vegetables for the sadza tonight. People should be given warning so they have a few moments to prepare themselves. To shut the animals in, milk the cows, bring in a bit of dry firewood and pick vegetables for dinner. Move nearer to me, my dear child."

Chinongwa automatically obeyed by swinging her body in the direction she was supposed to move, while not moving at all.

"Oh my dears, this rain. Look how it pours. And the size of the hailstones!"

She prattled on some more until Shorai contributed, "We saw roofs being blown into the valley, but yours seem to be still on.

It must be strong. Musiki has pointed us to the right home." Shorai looked up at the roof she could hardly see. Silently, she prayed for it to hold. Though it was leaking everywhere, at least it was a roof.

"The roof leaks and you are going to get just as wet as if you were outside," the woman continued. "I told the man who thatched it that it was going to leak because he talked while doing it. The more you talk, the more it leaks. His roofs leak. Move over, my dear child, don't be shy or you will catch a cold."

This time Chinongwa did move, though the improvement was slight.

"Thank heavens you were here when it started. Nobody can survive such a downpour. Today the cattle are going to sleep in the fields. The boys will never be able to drive them back to the pen. Look at the size of the stones. Tomorrow we shall send the children to see if they can find a few hares lying around. Or even small antelope. Stones this size can kill even decent-sized animals."

Masking the discomfort she felt because of the unexpected visitors, she fought the fire, which was stubbornly refusing to take. Between two phrases, she knelt this way and that, blew here and there, poked twigs and, in between, wiped tears from her eyes or blew her nose on her wet skirt.

Shorai went to the opposite side of the fire, blowing and poking while grunting agreement to what was being said.

"But this is not constructive rain. What sins have we committed to deserve this punishment? And yet we brewed the rukoto." The hostess stopped blowing and looked at Shorai, demanding an answer.

Shorai shrugged her shoulders. "Who knows? Only they, the gone ones, can tell us. They are not going to destroy us. They need us as much as we need them. Who will brew them beer to quench their thirst?"

The hostess suddenly stopped and looked at Shorai as if she had just discovered a truth. "You're right, they need us. Then it must be the new rain man. The old one is now blind and has passed his hand on to his son, who must have forgotten to mention we did not want thunder and lightning, floods, droughts and hailstorms. Every undesirable detail must be mentioned. But then it's his first time."

Shorai kept punctuating the hostess's mumbling. She accepted her excuses for the storm and reassured her that the smoke was not bothering them at all, even though everybody was in tears. She thought of offering snuff, but hers was wet and the hostess seemed too agitated. She was not sure what to do, for up to then there had not been any introductions. She decided to wait for the hostess to take the lead.

Baba Marehwa, seeing that there were no men in the hut, did not join in the women's talk, but he made positive noises whenever Shorai reassured the hostess.

"If the children had told me there were no more twigs under the hozi, I would have done it yesterday. But then children, ha, you know them. 'The child expert is the one who does not have one.' So there, today we are going to cry and cry before there is any fire in here."

On the far and opposite side of the door appeared a girl who looked two or three summers older than Chinongwa. In silence, she started rearranging the twigs. She did not seem as desperate as the hostess, nor did it seem to bother her that the fire kept dying. She blew at it without conviction. Chinongwa observed her closely, wanting to tell her to keep at it, but of course she could not.

The hostess was accustomed to having guests. When the Marehwa family appeared, she mistook them for her husband's guests. Patients would have been the right word, for her husband was a n'anga, known far and wide. At any time of the day and night, people with all kinds of ailments, physical or psychological, arrived. But even after the patients had stated their affairs, tradition demanded they be addressed as guests. This was done to avoid embarrassment if one mistook guests for patients. The Marehwa family did not know where they had landed and they kept waiting for the hostess to introduce herself and share snuff with them.

The hostess started apologising for her husband's absence. "Baba Chitsva is not here and I'm not sure when he will be back." She explained that the chief's messenger had turned up two days before and ordered her husband to accompany him. The chief's youngest wife had started again and there was nobody else but Baba Chitsva who could calm her down. Even if it hadn't been the chief's wife, he still would have gone. He never refused patients. And whenever he went to the chief, there was no telling when he would be back.

"I hope your matter is not too pressing. Do you think you can wait for him? It depends on what ails you."

When they told her that they had been out trying to find a husband for their young girl, she felt relieved they were not patients; but they were still guests and she had to look after them. Even at her age, she had never ceased to be frightened by thunder, but responsibilities demanded serenity. At least outwardly. She could tremble inside but she was not to show her fear, especially to guests. Right now, she had to go out in the rain to fetch some pumpkin leaves for supper, for she was not going to give the guests sadza with sour milk. Though the hailstones had ceased, the rain continued mercilessly.

Excusing herself, she leapt out into the rain where she was greeted with lightning and thunder in such close succession that at first she wasn't sure if she had just been struck. She could feel the vibrations in her chest. Her waters started running but she wasn't worried about that. She was already soaking wet.

As usual, during thunderstorms, she couldn't help seeing the dead body of the boy whom she'd once loved. Whether or not he had loved her as much as she did him was beside the point. But when he was struck by lightning, her childhood and all its dreams had died with him. They said the lightning had been sent by one of his father's brother's wives who was a muroyi. Up until the death of that woman, Mai Chitsva had hated her.

She acknowledged that she was still in love with him, or at least the girl in her was still in love with the idea or the memory of him. But during a storm like this, it was always his dead body that she saw, and it reinforced her fear of lightning. She made her way to the anthill. It was a long way, but in this downpour it was the only place where she would be able to pick any leaves that were not swimming in mud.

"When I get back, if the cattle are not yet in, I'll have to leave the guests to look for the boys and the cattle. No one should be out in this rain, let alone children. Still, if they had run them in the moment they felt the first drops, they might just have had enough time. But I shan't say anything … as soon as the guests know that they're not the fruits of my womb, they might assume that I don't care for them. That's always the problem when the children are not yours. Everybody watches and waits for you to make a false move, then they pounce like a cat on an unsuspecting rat. If only Baba Chitsva were here today. He would have gone to bring the cattle home when the storm began. I hope it drove the hyenas and jackals to the other side of the mountain. Tomorrow there won't be any calves left if the beasts spend the night in the woods."

She had to hurry. She was not going through the tomato field even though she had seen some ripe ones yesterday. They had to go without. Cattle were more important. She was not even going inside to excuse herself to the guests. She would just drop the vegetables at the door and run off.

She was startled when, on dropping the vegetables at the door and shouting to her niece—"Shamhu, start peeling the pumpkin leaves and get them ready!"—she saw Tawa, her younger stepson, coming in with dry grass for the fire.

"Where were the cattle heading for when you left them?"

74

"But we have shut them in already."

She was so relieved she thanked him with the totem as if he were an adult, "Thank you of the Shava totem, thank you, man of the house. May Musiki bless you with many children. Now give me the grass and I shall make the fire and get some food for you. It's a woman's duty to do that. Go and take a rest."

Tawa went inside looking puzzled. They had shut the cattle in as soon as the wind had risen. Due to an argument, the boys had not been speaking to each other but skulking around the kraals at shut-in time. They had milked the cows earlier than usual, prayed that it rained and, at the first hint, had shut in the cattle and run inside, congratulating themselves while hoping 'Mother' would never find out. Their argument had been swiftly forgotten.

Relieved, the old woman went to change her clothes and decided, now that everything else was in order, to make up for all the mishaps of the day. When she came into the cooking hut, she saw that the fire, with the help of Shorai, had finally taken. There was a warm glow, which filled her heart with goodwill that she threw all around. The chickens were shut in, the cows had been milked, the vegetables were there and the fire had taken. Even the storm had loosened its anger and there was no more rain leaking onto the guests' laps.

She passed snuff to her guests and discharged Shamhu from cooking. Once in a while, she would send an order to bring in more firewood, mealie-meal and salt, and the children took care of it. It was not until after the meal was finished and all the children had been sent off to sleep that the subject of Chinongwa was raised.

"If only Baba Chitsva were here, he would know what to do. How could they all refuse her? A woman should never be refused. They do not know how quickly a woman can flower and surprise all."

Shorai found herself excusing the same people that she had been cursing only that morning. "After the cattle disease

75

vasinamabvi brought with them, we don't have as many beasts as we once did. The world is no longer the same and many do not have enough food for themselves."

Though neither Baba Marehwa nor Shorai mentioned that they had already passed by when the husband was there and he had politely pointed them to someone else, they both wondered why he could be of any help a few days later. The subject of Chinongwa was to them both tiresome and unfortunate and, as far as they were concerned, better left alone. In any case, though they were not willing to discuss it with their hostess, the problem had already been solved—to nobody's satisfaction, for sure, but still solved.

Whenever there was thunder and lightning and she thought of her boy lover, Mai Chitsva always felt unfaithful to her husband; a husband who did not ask her to produce children for him even though he had paid cows that were still walking in her father's kraal; a husband to whom she felt she should be grateful. During the meal, the sensation abated, and after the snuff was passed she found herself relaxing. Although her husband was absent, she felt her goodwill stretching to wherever he was. She wanted it to touch him as well. And that was how it came, and it came without warning:

"If you trust me," she heard herself saying, "I can take the child and give her to my husband."

Both brother and sister, who had not shared their decision with their hostess out of shame of washing their dirty clothes in public, were dumbfounded. Neither knew what to say. Shorai could not say anything without first hearing her brother's opinion, but Baba Marehwa's thoughts were doing somersaults and his tongue was stuck to the ceiling of his mouth.

The hostess, who was now less sure of her feelings, was regretting the rash offer she had made and was fighting the need to bite off her loose tongue. She wondered if her guests had heard. Maybe it was not too late to pretend she had said something else.

Their faces were blank and they kept staring at her and each other. The silence became so oppressive she felt compelled to break it. It was getting embarrassing. So she launched into her life story:

"I was married to a wonderful man of good family and breeding. I lived with him for more than ten seasons without my womb opening. We went everywhere, saw everybody from far and wide. I tasted the roots of every tree. I ate and drank every grub that could be thought of, and in every imaginable position and at different times of the day and night. But nothing. I met my present husband when my first one brought me to him for consultation about my sterility. He saw right away that I could never bear a man a child. My womb was tied in knots. He told my husband that it was no use."

"Now, who would have thought that these children are not from your uterus?" Shorai directed this question at her brother, to whom she was also asking, "What do I say now?" Her brother knew no better and shrugged his shoulders, while grunting surprise that the children did not belong to the hostess.

The latter, unaware of all this, continued with her story. "And to think that it was he who gave me the simplest things to do. Just some gruel at sunrise. If I vomited, then I could have children, if nothing happened, then my womb was dead. I drank, nothing happened, and here I am. I could no longer keep my head high in the village. His parents did not stop reproaching me for having wasted their son's time. Many in the village suffered with me and many gave me advice or names of healers they knew, and although my husband loved me and would have wanted to keep me, he was going to have to marry another woman, and so I decided to leave. I have nothing against my ex-husband. He loved me. Ten seasons is a long time to wait for the womb of a woman to open. He was a man among men."

Baba Marehwa clapped his hands in praise of the ex-husband. "Yes, it does warm the heart, my mother, to hear that there are people like him. Too many times do we see what brings sores to the eyes and hear what brings pus to the ears. Yes, this is a good thing to be told, is it not, my mother's one?"

Shorai agreed, wondering if her brother was telling her that it was good to give Chinongwa to the hostess. She fixed her eyes on him and decided that the nodding could only mean she was right, but then he was not smiling or looking happy.

"When my ex-husband's people brought him another wife, I ran back to my people. When he kept coming to see me to persuade me to go back to him, I ran away to my present husband, who had told me that I could come whenever I wanted. His previous wife had died after the birth of their third child. When I turned up at the good man's, he fetched his munyai, selected five head of cattle and told him to take them to my people. One for my mother who was still alive and the rest was danga. I cried with pride and gratitude. I have never cried so much in happiness."

"Of course, there was reason to cry with happiness. It is not every day that luck like that falls onto one's lap, is that not true, my brother?" Shorai looked at her brother's face with anxiety. How come he did not seem to appreciate the sudden turn in their fortunes?

"When my brothers saw the munyai arrive with the cattle, they could understand nothing and came to explain to Baba Chitsva that I could not have any children. He told them that I already had children, his children. He was going to pay for me just like he would pay for a maiden. And, for the second time, my mother received her mother's cow. My mother never received two mother's cows for my two sisters who have homes full of children. All this, thanks to me, the sterile … Me, who nobody respects because I am barren."

"One should never say things like that. Why, there are many people who do not merit half the respect that you do, mother. I would not talk like that." Baba Marehwa did not refer his answer to Shorai and she felt more confused. Was her brother saying the hostess was a better person than her?

"If my sisters-in-law had any respect, should they not give him one of their daughters to compensate for me, who can never give him heirs? I know my brothers respect my husband and that, if the matter was up to them only, they would have long ago presented him with a maiden. But do you ever hear him complain? Never, not Baba Chitsva."

This was directed at Baba Marehwa, who vigorously nodded his head to show he understood. The flames of the fire were dying down and they could not see Mai Chitsva's face very well, but her dry and clear voice held them captive.

"My father, when he realised that I could never conceive, had decided to give my ex-husband his roora back, but he refused it. I have been living with Baba Chitsva, who knows everything about me and does not expect anything of a woman. I am telling you this, a subject I never talk about except to those that I hold here." She placed her two palms, one over the other, over her heart. She looked first at the sister and then at the brother, and both, if they had had doubts, now understood that she was indeed serious.

Afraid to break the magic, they nodded back without saying a word. They were not thinking about Chinongwa but listening, spellbound.

"Since my husband is still young, I think it will be a good idea if he could have more children. I know that my family has decided not to reward my husband for his good heart, but I'm ready to reward him myself."

Brother and sister stared at her, mesmerised.

Shorai was no longer looking at her brother for instructions. She decided that if ever there were instructions, they were going to come from this woman sitting beside her. This woman knew what was to be done; one had only to obey her and all would be well.

Baba Marehwa, who at first had been suspicious, wondering if his sister had not had a hand in this, was now all ears, all doubts gone. Though he was not proud to take charity from his sister, he had managed to convince himself that there was something wrong with his daughter—and until he went to a n'anga to find out, nobody, including her sister's husband, was going to touch her.

"The two boys are his children and the girl is his sister's, and I raise them as my own. If you leave your daughter here, I shall treat her as my own, just like the others. And when the time comes, I shall have prepared her for her role. The cattle pen is bursting. You could drive away five or six head tomorrow and you will be able to exchange them for millet when you reach home."

At the mention of cattle and millet, brother and sister suddenly brightened up at the thought of arriving with food. Baba Marehwa could not hide his contentment and joy. He felt some weight fall off.

Shorai, understanding his brother's thoughts, felt like ululating, dancing, hugging the hostess. Only good breeding held her back. Could it be true or was it a dream? Was she going to wake up feeling cheated? She had a calm countenance that fooled the others, but if one had looked at her eyes, her fast pumping heart was mirrored in them. She had been sitting cross-legged and now stretched her feet in front of her, took out her snuff horn and, without a word, stretched out her hand to her hostess, who, without a word, stretched out her left palm for the snuff. And then she did the same for her brother, who took his without saying a word either. Chinongwa's fate was sealed thus.

The three adults slept better than they had done for a long time. Shorai had once more got back her dear husband, who wasn't like all the others, and she reconciled herself with her wonderful niece, whom she now loved more than she had ever done before. She also felt a tinge of guilt for having blamed Chinongwa for events that she couldn't control. Baba Marehwa felt the yoke loosen around his neck and breathed more easily; he was not going to be forever indebted to his younger sister and he was going to leave Chinongwa in good hands and at a respectable distance from home. The hostess felt that deep within her that she had finally atoned for having secretly loved a boy who was not her husband. She was sacrificing a virgin. Even if she might one day suffer for it, today she felt cleansed and pure. She did not rule out the possibility that, because she was giving a virgin to her husband, one day her womb might open and she would finally be a woman.

Chinongwa, oblivious to these events, slept on.

10

Chinongwa had expected to be woken at the second cock's crow as usual. Mostly, it was Tete Shorai who woke her. Instead, today it was Shamhu, the girl, with whom she had slept in the hozi. Yes, it was normal that at first she couldn't recollect where she was. In the last few days, it had been hard to know where she found herself every morning.

What was not normal today was to be gently woken. No whispering or dragging. What was happening? The birds were already exchanging greetings outside and from the sound of it they had been at it for ages. She could hear the calves crying out to their mothers and the cows calling back.

Suddenly, she realised that while her mind had been trying to find meaning in all this confusion, Shamhu had been speaking to her. She was asking if she minded going to the well to fetch some water. She quickly agreed and both jumped out of the hozi and took the zvirongo that were kept under the hozi. But just as they came out, Chinongwa decided that she could not go with Shamhu since she was not sure if they weren't leaving right away, late as it was, so she asked Shamhu to wait a moment.

She headed for the cooking hut where she found her aunt and the hostess peacefully breaking their fast with some of the leftover sadza from the previous evening. Before she could guess the meaning of this, Tete Shorai greeted her with a wide smile that she did not remember ever having seen before. "Did you sleep well, my father's one? You look well. Now, say good morning to Amaiguru. She is our Amaiguru, my dear child. And now you go with Shamhu and get us water. I saw both of you with zvirongo. What happened?"

With this encouragement, Chinongwa left the cooking hut to join her new friend. Though she kept grunting in answer to what Shamhu was saying, Chinongwa's mind was worlds away. She was trying to decipher what had taken possession of Tete Shorai. Why was her aunt in such a happy mood? She had just called her "my father's one". Though they both shared the same paternal roots, Tete Shorai had always behaved as if she regretted the link. But today?

And all this after what had happened yesterday before the storm: though not many words had been exchanged, Shorai had hinted at what the new arrangement would be and had made it clear that she was not at all pleased to share her husband. Chinongwa had been worried ever since and was trying to find a way to refuse the match. Yet, this morning, she could tell that yesterday's storm had washed something away and brought in something new. Today's Tete Shorai was not the same woman. But what had changed? She did not know whether she should go into mourning or celebrate.

The storm had wrought destruction as far as the eye could see, and presently Shamhu, who was in front of her, was commenting on the huge hailstones that had rained on them the day before. She had never seen such big ones. Though Chinongwa could see the naked trees and their shredded leaves, and though in the whole of her short life she had never seen such a hailstorm either, she did not appreciate the situation. She walked on the carpet of dead leaves as if it had been laid out for her.

As far as she could remember, they had stopped there not because they knew the people but because of the storm. And yet Tete Shorai had just told her that the woman was their Amaiguru. Her immediate occupation was to find out if she was related on her mother's or father's side. She suspected she had seen her before, but could not be sure. She had met so many lost members of the family. If she was their Amaiguru, how come it hadn't been mentioned the night before, during the meal or after?

On the way back from the well with her chirongo balanced on her head, as she mechanically followed Shamhu, her senses were sharp, to anything unusual. She felt something in the air. The bright cloudless sky seemed to reinforce the idea of a new world. The storm providing the snapping point between two worlds. And, despite all her anxieties, today had begun with an unnaturally long sleep, a wide smile from an unexpected corner and a bright new day, but one that felt suspiciously different.

She felt her spirits rise, lightening her heart and pushing her forward. The cool morning wind blew noiselessly through the stripped branches. The wet leaves that carpeted the path seemed to cleanse her feet of the past and prepare her for a new life. Everything seemed clearer, cleaner and well defined, and yet she could not be sure why. She was convinced that it was linked to the smile that her aunt had given her. It had been a real one, and Chinongwa had smiled back before she realised what she was doing. That, in itself, was a big event, and a worry. Were all these positive signs a good omen or a facade for something more sinister?

Shamhu's voice cut into her reverie, the girl kept interrupting. Suddenly, a fear and a need to know gripped her, and she hurried forward with the excitement that was bubbling inside her. She had to take another look at her aunt's face. Now! She overtook Shamhu, who was taken aback by this apparently silent girl whom she had tried to talk to but who had refused to respond. Not to be outdone, Shamhu also increased her pace, and so both girls arrived, almost running, their zvirongo balanced on their heads, giggling and out of breath. Shamhu felt satisfied that she had finally managed to connect with the girl, though she had not said anything, at least she had laughed.

The adults were surprised and pleased that the girls had not taken forever. To rid themselves of the forever demanding adults, young girls always took their time at the well. Even though they were always rebuked for the time they took, the little break seemed worth it; and because every mother had felt the same way, it was always forgiven.

"Thank you, thank you, vasikana. But, look at its colour! You would think someone had put milk into it. I'm sure it's because of Chinongwa that they came back so quickly; Shamhu never hurries. I shout at her but even then …"

The hostess was helping Chinongwa take the chirongo off her head and putting it on the chikuva.

"Oh no, Amaiguru, I am sure it was Shamhu who hurried them along, Chinongwa is always slow to return from the well." Shorai returned the compliment to her hostess with such amity that one might have believed she'd known her all her life.

Amaiguru ordered the girls to go wash the dishes from the evening before. As they left, Shamhu was burbling about what else they might do, but Chinongwa was reluctant to go too far away. Her father was not anywhere in sight, so it was only by watching her aunt and maybe Amaiguru that she could hope to find out what had changed the atmosphere. So, instead of washing the pots with Shamhu, she kept popping in and out of the cooking hut, pretending to look around for dirty dishes, while capturing fragments of conversation.

When Shorai threw her the 'get out and be scarce' look, she went out only to come back immediately to hear Shorai telling Amaiguru, "I'm leaving you a lot of work, Amaiguru. You always have to be behind her. If not, nothing gets done. Don't hesitate to correct her, she's still a child. I leave everything in your capable hands, my sister."

Shaken, Chinongwa was about to return outside when she discovered that Shamhu had been standing beside her, also listening to the conversation. And although Shorai could see them, she did not chase them away. She continued as if they were not there.

"You're going to be her tete and her mother. Where I left off, you will pick up. I have complete confidence in you. Yes, I have, or I would not be leaving her here. She's my own flesh and blood, after all." Both girls looked at each other and went outside.

Chinongwa quickly sat down, her back to the wall of the hut in case her legs gave in. A cold shiver ran up her spine and she shuddered.

As far as she could remember, she had always been a subject of conversation, plans, projections and arguments. When she was smaller, she had mostly ignored the talk, but ever since Muraswa was given away her feelings had been of anger, desperation, shame and guilt. When for the first time she knew that they were taking her to look for a husband, she had wet herself, but never before had she felt this sensation of dread.

Yesterday, when she had understood that she was going to be given to Tete Shorai's husband, she had felt no shiver at all, only anger, and a sudden determination to fight them all as soon as they returned home. She was not going to accept living and sharing a husband with her aunt. She was going to shame them all and they were going to be surprised by her strength. They were going to have to bring her to him tied hand and foot.

But that was yesterday and the ground had looked familiar. Today, the situation had drastically changed. The revolt and energy of yesterday was replaced by a fatal acceptance and resignation. She felt numb in mind and body, as if her blood had stopped flowing and her nerves had gone dead. She felt tired, helpless, lost. It did not seem to matter any more what happened now.

Shamhu, who didn't have the faintest clue of what was going on, decided that Chinongwa must be a patient and was going to be left there for her uncle to examine. Had she understood how her uncle was supposed to 'have a look' at her new friend, maybe she wouldn't have felt so happy to have a girl of nearly her own age to talk to, play with and share some of the household chores. Even if the girl was only a patient, it didn't matter. Most of her uncle's patients were adults or small children or babies. She hoped that he would be able to cure Chinongwa from her muteness. Shamhu had understood that though the girl did not say anything, she was definitely not deaf. She now hoped that she might not be cured too quickly and leave. Shamhu decided that she didn't even mind if Chinongwa stayed mute, as long as she had a friend around. She had always dreamt of having a sister.

When her two cousins, Tawa and Wangi, played, they often excluded her from their games unless she was willing to play the wife of the brave hunter, or a dog or cow. And whenever she proposed a game, they would not play it with her because it was not for boys. Only when one of the cousins was absent was she allowed to play a hunter or brave soldier. She knew that were it not for Wangi, Tawa would not mind playing with girls. As long as he did not get caught. Whenever Tawa was playing with Shamhu and he saw Wangi or some of his friends arrive, he would slink off. She knew that Tawa was her friend and Wangi was not. She was never sure, though, whether, with Wangi, if it was simply because she was a girl or because she did not really belong. That her father was unknown was a shame to her and her family and she had never been able to ascertain whether that was the reason Wangi disliked her. Everybody knew that her mother had had her without being married and had never divulged the name of her lover.

Another mystery was how Shamhu had stuck to the uterus of her mother, in spite of whatever her mother had drunk, eaten or done to get rid of her. Even when her mother could not hide her pregnancy any longer and was beaten to near death by her brother, Baba Chitsva, Shamhu had hung on. A healthier baby was seldom delivered in the village. Her mother called her Shamhu, in memory of the ten switches that her brother had laid on her body. Four seasons after her birth, her mother left to marry a very rich man who did not know that Shamhu existed. Shamhu, like Tawa and Wangi, called her own mother tete. Though her uncle and aunt were good to her and treated her like their own child, Shamhu could not help wishing she had a normal family, complete with father, mother, brothers and sisters. Her innermost wish was to be able to call someone 'mother', but she had long ago been made to understand that she would be putting her mother's marriage at risk if ever her husband discovered the truth. As she grew older, she came to understand her mother's situation. The more she understood, the more she felt ashamed. She consoled herself by thanking Musiki for making her a female. A nameless male is even worse.

But, for the time being, Shamhu felt lucky she was finally going to be able to play some of those games that Tawa and Wangi would never be caught playing. And she sincerely hoped that they were going to be as jealous of her as she was of them.

Meanwhile, both girls finished cleaning the dishes, while the two women finalised the details.

Seeing Chinongwa lost in thought, Shamhu decided to tell her about her plans to make the boys jealous. "We shall tell them they are not allowed to play with us or even watch. We can play brides and let them watch, but we don't want them to be our husbands."

89

She realised it was energy lost, for there was no reaction. She looked at Chinongwa again and decided that she must surely be right that the girl had come for treatment and maybe she was really sick. How could anyone be shivering so?

To Chinongwa, whose eyes were open but unseeing, Shamhu's voice seemed to be coming from a long way off. Everything that Shamhu was saying sounded disjointed and the words did not make sense. She was too tired to care to understand.

And maybe she is possessed too, Shamhu thought. After all, that is why they are leaving her here, isn't it? She definitely has horrible spirits roughing her up. Still, I'm sure she will get better soon once Sekuru gets back. With this, Shamhu gave up trying to make contact and decided to wait for the bad spirits to be driven away before she tried again.

Some time later, the two girls were given their breakfast and Chinongwa, who was coming back to herself, sat beside Shamhu and ate with an outside calm as if it was another day. The shivering had finally stopped. Now she knew her destiny, her body relaxed. She felt she could finally breathe without effort. It was as if she had been hanging in limbo without her feet touching the ground.

Her mind went to her future family-in-law; her mother-in-law, sister-in-law and the two boys, one of whom was surely going to be her husband. She had not yet met her future father-in-law, so she decided to examine him when the time came. She looked at those present. The first was Shamhu, who, unaware of Chinongwa's eyes on her, was prattling on about cucumbers that were big enough to be eaten, promising to show them to Chinongwa. And while she talked, she threw small pieces of food to the hens and chicks that were pecking at her legs and feet. This was the first time Chinongwa had ever seen anyone playing with food. In her village, food was sacred and was never thrown in fun to animals or birds. But here even the hens did not seem to be particularly grateful for the morsels and took their time to decide whether to eat them.

Chinongwa was scandalised. If she was not going to be my sister-in-law, she thought, I would have told her what I think of people who play with their food. But then I owe her just as much respect as I owe my future husband. I'm going to be the muroora, and though I'm sure I'm more mature than her, I have to respect her. I am a Marehwa and Marehwas are well brought up. I'm not going to be angry with her. After all, they have a lot of food, so what does it matter if she throws scraps to the hens? Had she known of Shamhu's position in the family, it would have softened her heart.

Her thoughts then turned to the two boys. They are, both of them, older than me, of that I am nearly sure. By two summers? Three? I wonder which one is going to be my husband. If I'd known, I would have looked at them more closely last night. They resemble each other, but the older brother's ears stand out from his head a little. If they ask me, I shall not know which one to choose. I hope they're not going to ask me today. Even if I'd paid more attention to them last night, I'm not sure I would know. They were sitting on the bench quite far from the fire, so how could I have been able to see them clearly? And they were speaking to each other in whispers.

That morning she had not seen them either and she was not sure she could recognise them in a crowd. She kept looking out in the hope of seeing them without being seen.

Ambuya said a bride should not look at one's groom, she reminded herself, but keep her eyes averted. Maybe they're hiding and examining me without my knowing. I hope not! I wish my skirt was cleaner.

At the same time, she desperately wanted them to be good husbands and could imagine them only in that light. No beatings such as those she'd heard of. I'll be an obedient wife, a good mother, a generous daughter-in-law. And why not? I'll love the man I marry. Anything is better than marrying Tete Shorai's husband.

Because she could not separate the two boys in her mind, she kept thinking of her husband in the plural. They were one faceless body. As such thoughts filled her head, she was pretending to listen and grunting automatically in answer to Shamhu's questions and explanations.

Lastly, she examined the woman she thought of as her future mother-in-law. She had a pleasant-enough face, she decided. The huge gap in the middle of her upper row of teeth is a sign of generosity. But she had been more than impressed by the woman's size. She was the biggest woman she had ever seen, too big for comfort. She was both tall and broad, and Chinongwa felt slightly overwhelmed. Anyone so beautiful and with such a wide gap in the teeth cannot be wholly cruel, no matter how large she is, she reassured herself.

11

Even if it had not been so wet, the village wouldn't have done any weeding that day. Chinongwa's arrival had broken the usual day-to-day routine. Early that morning, Mai Chitsva had asked Baba Mashava, their alcoholic neighbour, to kill a pig for the guests.

She then sent the boys to invite the villagers to come and meet the newcomers, not forgetting to remind them to keep an eye out for any hares killed by the storm. This they did after milking the cows so as to catch everybody before they left for the fields. Though the village was not large—three tens and a few more fires in all—the families were scattered over the area. Only from the hilltop could one see all the huts. To the east of the Chitsva compound, from where Baba Marehwa, his sister and daughter had arrived the evening before, lay the headman and his family's compound. His nearest neighbour was even further east and his compound could only just be seen through the huge musasa trees that provided welcome shade. Most of the village was located to the west behind the hill and most huts followed the river at a distance as it occasionally flooded though it was always an important source of water for animals and villagers.

***

Along the river, on both sides, was lush woodland where fig trees knew no season and provided the villagers with fruit all year round. Some parts deeper inside the forest were so dense that even when an injured antelope hid away from the pursuing hunters, most men chose to return home empty-handed rather than venture into the dark forests. During the winter when the river was low, men crossed to the other side to harvest honey from the hives they had placed in the trees the year before.

These were a lucky people, the first settlers in the area and a relatively small group, so they had more than enough land for their crops and beasts. The soil was a rich red clay and gave generously to those who cared to turn and weed it three times before the harvest. Every year the soil was further enriched by the termites that worked it with their sharp jaws and supplied the villagers with their fat bodies at the beginning of the rains.

It took the boys the whole morning to reach everybody.

Tawa started with the headman and his dog announced his arrival as he came to see what the noise was all about. "Ah, good morning. Is it not you, Chitsva? Now, which one are you, Tawa or Wangi?"

"Good morning, yes, I am Tawa. Wangi is the older one."

"And how did you sleep, Vakuru?" The boys politely exchanged the formal greetings.

"Ah, at my age one cannot sleep well. There is the back that does not stop complaining. I listen to the first, then the second, then the third cock crow, and I know that soon the bulbul will start its morning greetings. You will see when you reach my age. And

94

last night, all was compounded by the worry brought about by the storm. How can anyone sleep well? How did your parents sleep?"

"Well, thank you. My mother wanted you to bless her with your family's company once the sun has dried the dew."

"Ah, she wants my company, does she? Can't you whisper in my ear what for? Or are you not allowed?"

"No, I'm not allowed. Do I tell her that you will bless her?"

"Of course, of course, child. We shall all be there. Give her my greetings."

The boys had been instructed to explain nothing, but just inform the villagers that their presence was wanted as there were guests at home. If pressed for more information, they explained how many guests there were and whether or not they were adults, men or women. Since they did not know more than this, the inquiries ended there and the boys would then be free to go to the next family, where a similar scenario was played out.

By the time the sun was overhead, almost the whole village had arrived at Mai Chitsva's homestead. The elderly ate inside while the younger ate outside, sitting on rocks or logs. As befitted the occasion, red millet sadza was cooked outside in huge clay pots and served with the roasted pig.

After the food had been consumed, there was a convocation in the cooking hut, where Mai Chitsva announced her decision, "Relatives and friends, it is I who has assembled you here to witness my decision. It has now been ten seasons since you received me here. I know that when I came, many of you expected me to produce something, but when my womb did not open there was talk." The ten seasons were demonstrated by her ten fingers, held out for them all to see. In response, all eyes were fixed on the floor and there were muffled mumbles of shame and denial from the audience, but Mai Chitsva continued her charge. "Yes, there was talk. Tongues wagged, hot-peppered tongues that brought out scalding words. I know some of the names that you gave me, but

I didn't listen or worry. Why should I have cared, as long as my master was standing by me? I was immune to this kind of baseness and I watched you with a knowing smile while I waited for the storm to abate."

There was less murmuring this time, but heads and eyes continued to stare intently at the floor. "Then the tongues got tired of wagging and the minds forgot, but mine did not do so. My womb still has not opened and it will not open tomorrow, but my master is good, and he is young. This decision I take freely on my own without any pressure from anybody, least of all my master. He is a selfless man and I have decided to reward him. When he comes back from curing the chief's wife, he will find that I have taken a maiden for him and, in a few seasons, he will have more children to fill this home as he deserves. So there, my older ones, this is my excuse for assembling you here today and making you leave your homes and your work."

Then there was silence, a silence that nobody dared interrupt. When it became unbearable, the headman's wife started ululating and, relieved, all stood up and started dancing and singing songs of praise. And down the cheeks of Mai Chitsva ran hot tears of longing for a child that would not come, of relief for having at last said what was innermost, and love for all these people, who first refused her and then accepted her as she was.

After the singing and dancing, word came back from the headman, whose eyes were still trained on the floor between his feet. "Yes, there was talk, as there is always talk, otherwise what are our tongues for? But let it be known that it is not always of the bad kind. Sometimes it is in one's honour or one's husband's honour. Also, it must never be forgotten that one's suffering is many others' suffering, and one's joy is many others' joy too. 'That one with a long nose will always think that everyone is talking about it.' At the same time, let us not rejoice in other people's sufferings, for what do we gain from it except ugliness and decay of body and mind?

But enough of that. Today, let us rejoice. And let us not suffer, forever saying we have not produced from our womb—for what one has in this home, are they not children? And if one is not the mother, who is then? Do they have any other except this one we see? Who has cooked for them all these ten seasons? Who bathes them and spends sleepless nights looking after them whenever they are sick?"

The headman lifted his eyes off the floor and directed them at Mai Chitsva. "When people pass through here, would they ever suspect that these are not products of your womb? Even when one looks in the village, how many mothers compete with you? We have eyes to see and ears to hear. And we also have hearts, and they are thankful. We all know that inside that body there, there is a heart bigger than many."

This speech was greeted with more applause and ululating from the women, more tears from Mai Chitsva and the ebbing of tension inside the hut.

The headman continued, "And hear me, all of you," and here he raised his voice and stuck his chest out. He was not the headman now, just another man, and his speech was addressed to all the women present, "How many of you would do what we are witnessing today? How many times have we heard of that jealous woman who has poured hot water on the new bride that her husband has just brought, or scratched her left eye out, or burnt her hut while she is sleeping inside, or chopped off her left arm or leg? This act we are here witnessing stems from a woman with a heart to spare, one overflowing with love, respect, trust, gratitude, giving and charity. This here is an example of the perfection of womanhood. I could go on until sunset."

After a while, the villagers asked to see Chinongwa, who was presently brought into the hut. She was introduced just as "the story that I have just related to you, my elders." A stony silence followed her entrance. She sat down by Shorai. If she had been a cow, she would have been swiftly refused. This audience consisted of those lucky ones who had run away with their full herds when vasinamabvi had arrived. They had managed to find plentiful and fertile land to settle on. They could not imagine the suffering of those who had lost land, herd and flock, and the vision in front of them, as far as most of them were concerned, could only be explained by one thing: laziness.

After all these days of walking Chinongwa was not at her best. Her mother's old skirt was dirty, discoloured and muddy at the bottom. Her eyes had not been cleaned for two days. Her face had not been washed that morning. When she was called into the hut, she had just started eating and had not been able to wash her hands, so she had just wiped her hands on her skirt. Just before she went in, she had remembered her nose and wiped it with the back of her right hand and managed to spread a little snot across her right cheek, stretching it from the nose to the ear. Mixed with the fat from the pig that she was eating, the effect could not have been worse.

When Shorai saw her niece enter, she wanted to disappear into the ground. Yes, Chinongwa had been accepted as she was, but Shorai was her aunt and this morning, in her rejoicing, she had forgotten to prepare her, and now she was being presented to the village. Everyone knew that Shorai was the tete. Yes, they were hungry people but they were not dirty. How could she have forgotten to prepare her? Even though she was being given away, it was Chinongwa's day and she, as the tete, should have made sure her niece looked her best. That was why her brother had brought her along. She should have gotten rid of that skirt and given Chinongwa her own head scarf instead. At least it was clean. What were all these people going to think of her? There was no way she could retrieve the situation. She kept her head down and prayed that Mai Chitsva was not going to speak to her.

When Baba Marehwa saw his daughter entering, his heart and head also sank. His gaze turned to his sister, and if looks could kill. He asked himself whether it had been worth the trouble bringing his sister if his daughter was to be presented like that. He wondered if she had not done it on purpose to shame him; to pay him back for the day before.

Mai Chitsva felt triumphant. The worse Chinongwa looked, the better her sacrifice was reflected. She felt her stature growing, felt her good and noble heart swell to double size. Not only had she taken a maiden to offer to her husband, but she had at the same time helped to feed a family.

Her immediate job would be to fill and fatten Chinongwa up and show all those people who disapproved of the girl on the basis of her current bony state. She was going to transform her, and these gossipy, miserable people were going to regret all they had said and thought. She was going to see to it, even if it became her reason for being.

None in the hut was left untouched. There were those who could not help feeling sorry for the little human in front of them. For those, the esteem and physical size of their hostess rose as they looked at Chinongwa. They felt small, heartless and lacking in humanity. Their hostess gave them hope for the future of humanity, but left them asking themselves if they could rise to such an occasion.

Then there were those who were moved to believe the rumours about landless people, but what they couldn't understand was why Mai Chitsva was involving herself with such people. Physical contact was out of the question. It made them feel lucky, and when they went back home they were going to work even harder so they would never be hungry and reduced to such a pitiful state. They were going to feed their children until they looked like fat little pigs ready for slaughter. They were going to put more millet into storage just in case.

Then there were those who were simply disgusted with Baba Marehwa, his sister and daughter. To them, these three lazybones were nothing but beggars who, not content to stay at home and eat their misery, were flaunting it and disturbing their tranquil lives by showing off their skinny daughter. They were angry at Mai Chitsva for dirtying their village by accepting the girl. What if more people from that lazy village started arriving with their starving offspring, thinking that they could marry them off here?

Lastly, there were all those men who, before seeing Chinongwa, had been imagining all sorts of things that could be done with a girl-wife. Now that they had the feast in front of them, many suddenly became fathers again and could not look at Chinongwa without thinking of their own children.

While all this was turning in people's minds, nobody took notice of the heavy silence that had fallen until Mai Chitsva cut in to tell Chinongwa that she could go and play outside. When Shorai heard these words, she could breathe once more, but still she could not raise her head. Sweat was running down her forehead, down her sides from under her arms, and she dared not wipe herself for fear of drawing attention to her discomfort.

In due time, eulogies were sung to the hostess and the afternoon passed peacefully while the village ate and sank into reminiscence. Cases were quoted, though everybody made sure to discuss positive examples of child brides. Stories of new wives that terminated in suicides or homicides were conveniently excluded. Today was a celebration and all felt duty-bound to enjoy it.

Until late, people kept dropping in and leaving though there was a lazy intermittent drizzle which felt as if it could go on for days. Then talk changed to the damage that the storm had wreaked, and there was fear that the harvest would not be as abundant as usual. The sight of Chinongwa and the reason why she had been brought to them reinforced their fears. Even though most crops were young enough to recover if it stopped raining, one could never be sure. When the subject became more ominous after a few references to Chinongwa's arrival heralding the storm, the subject was tactically changed to something more light-hearted. So even though there had been no preparation, Chinongwa's welcome was, in the last analysis, a festive one. Drums were brought in to accompany the singing and dancing inside the hut.

That evening, the headmen stayed on after everybody had left and, together with Baba Mashava and Baba Marehwa, he discussed how many cattle the Marehwas would take with them and when they should return for more millet. It was agreed that within two weeks Chinongwa's father would return with his sons for more grain and to meet his future son-in-law.

Though in front of the hostess all the villagers had manifested their approval of what she had done, in private there was a lot of tongue-wagging, even among the men. Although the men admired her for it and wished all women were as understanding, they didn't really understand it themselves—knowing nothing, of course, about Mai Chitsva's long-departed boy lover. And to relieve their heavy hearts, the women invited each other to head for the well where they could gossip to their hearts content, "Why dig one's own grave?" they asked. How could one destabilise one's situation so? While they admired such generosity, could it not have been directed towards more fitting causes? Of course her husband had only two children, but was it not better to leave things as they were? Especially since he had not asked for a younger wife. How many had been to him for consultation? How many owed him their lives? And how many had offered their daughters as compensation? How many times had he refused? If he had wanted a second wife, it was at the lift of a finger that one would have come running.

The headman's wife, though she had no co-wife, led the pack. "What if she comes from a family of sorcerers and witches well known in the village of origin? Why did the people of her village not marry her? Six days of walking? How can she be so sure this skeleton will not turn against her in the future? The elders say, 'If you bring up a dog on milk, tomorrow it will bite you.' She thinks she knows how to treat a man! We shall see who is going to pay the penalty."

They did not even pretend to hurry back. Most of them were sitting on the wet grass, laughing uneasily and in shrill tones. No second or third wives were present. The well did not belong to them today. The headman's wife continued, "Why did she not give him someone of her own blood? Does she not have a younger sister or a niece? It helps if it is one of your own because, whatever he does, the husband cannot divide the same blood. I had an uncle who decided that now he had the younger sister who had children, he did not need the older childless sister. He beat her up and told her to pack and go. Right away the younger sister also started her packing. You should have seen who went on the floor to grovel."

Mai Mashava did not agree. "But that's when everything goes well and the two sisters are intelligent, my dear one. I have cousins from my mother's side. The usual story. Older sister has three little children and can't cope alone, so little sister comes to help her out. And as soon as little sister's fruits appear and she starts to wash, like magic she keeps putting on weight and a few moons later what do we discover? Big sister asks younger sister if something is wrong and, of course, little sister is innocent. All she knows is how to play with the children. Big sister confronts her husband, who explains that it only happened once and it was the fault of little sister."

"Yes, it's always the woman's fault!" the women cried out in unison.

Mai Mashava continued. "Big sister had been told to watch out for small sister, but still she let the hyena take her. Shame on big sister. She had better go home and tell her parents that she neglected to look after her small sister. You know what my uncle and aunt said to her?"

"We have a rough idea," the headman's wife said.

"My uncle says, 'How could you let your husband do that to your own sister? Was he starved? Didn't you give him his daily food? Make sure he marries your sister, for what are we going to do with used goods? Who will want to marry her now?'"

While Mai Mashava imitated the characters in her story, the other women were rolling with laughter. "So she goes back to her husband and begs him to marry her younger sister because her parents think she neglected to look after the child. Can you believe it?" More laughter. "What does he say, 'As a man I shall have to sacrifice. I shall send the munyai tomorrow with a cow or two and save you from your parents' anger. Now I'm going to be a few cows poorer because your stupid young sister could not leave me alone.' Even though she knows that her husband raped her sister, what can she do except be grateful to the self-sacrificing husband? Three seasons later, he loves only the young wife, and when he caught a hare, instead of sharing it between the two women, he tied it in a tree near the well and told the younger one to bring it on her head as if carrying water. The older sister never knew better: so much for your same blood!"

Still the headman's wife was for one's own blood. "Yes, I know it happens if the younger sister is not intelligent, but I'd still go for my own blood. Your own sister might take the hare, but I don't think she would kill your hens or burn your sleeping hut while you're inside. But this girl is a complete stranger. We don't know where she comes from."

Then the toothless midwife, who was wisdom itself, lisped, "But don't forget that there were many families like us who lost everything and are now reduced to begging. So who knows? Maybe the skeleton is one of us. Though it's hard to understand that after all these seasons a family like us would still have nothing to eat. I don't believe that story. And tell me why the tete is not a heap of bones like her niece? There's a mystery in all this."

103

The headman's wife interjected, "I don't care what the mystery is. All I know is that Mai Chitsva, besides putting us in trouble for weeks, if not moons, because of her good heart, will live to regret this act. I'm not going to pretend that I'll feel sorry for her. Even if I were the husband, I would say 'no thank you', if that's her idea of a maiden. What a bag of bones!"

To this, all the women exploded in fits of laughter. It was difficult to tell whether their tears were of laughter, or anger at Mai Chitsva, who had somehow betrayed their code of conduct. They knew they were going to be hearing their husbands praising Mai Chitsva for a long time to come. Their husbands may even come home with young wives of their own after such a precedent.

But nobody asked why the sight of Chinongwa brought so much glee. They rushed to agree that they felt sorry for the girl, how sad they were for her and her mother, who must be suffering. In the same breath they laughed about her sore red eyes, her dirty clothes, and, most of all, her bony figure. They engaged themselves in an undeclared competition to give her a suitable nickname. Every one that was proposed was greeted with more laughter and objections were raised to its unsuitability until, finally, they agreed on Mapfupa—meaning 'bones'. The women, satisfied, filled their zvirongo and departed. But on her way home, without the support of the group, the headman's wife felt a certain disgust at her behaviour. She had discovered something ugly about herself that she hadn't known existed.

Meanwhile, Mai Chitsva was preparing dinner and reassuring herself that Chinongwa was never going to be as desirable to men as she was. She was accustomed to feeling good about herself. Even at her age, she was still capable of turning heads. Not bearing children of her own had one advantage; it made her look seasons younger than she really was. Although she was never going to hold her own in her arms and heal the wound that did not stop bleeding, there had always been some compensation in her misfortune.

That she had been born on the right side of looks had added to these advantages and helped to boost her confidence in herself even further. She also possessed an energy and strength that none of the women in the village of around her age could match: she could bring a pile of wood double the size that any of them could carry. She knew that the women in the village had nicknamed her 'Murume' because of her unusual strength, and that the name had come only because they were jealous.

So although Chinongwa had finally landed, she had landed on the wrong foot. And though she had arrived in a rainstorm and no bridal feast had been waiting for her, she had caused more upheaval in this quiet village than any bride had ever done. The storm was blamed on her as was the not-so-successful harvest that followed. The arrival of two new second wives two and three moons after her arrival also became her fault. To the village and surroundings, events were divided into those that happened before and those that happened after the arrival of Mapfupa. But Chinongwa thankfully remained oblivious to most of this.

12

Chinongwa did not cry when Baba Marehwa and Shorai left two days later. She watched them follow the path that divided the maize from the peanut patch, circumvent the well, pass the cattle pens and then disappear into the woods that bordered the village. Her father was in front, holding the three bast ropes that tied the three beasts through their horns, and her aunt was driving them from behind with a fresh branch. They did not turn back once as they departed. Tawa, Wangi, Shamhu and Mai Chitsva stood and watched them without speaking. They remained in the same position for some time after the visitors and the cattle could no longer be seen.

Chinongwa followed them in her mind through the woods and across the summer stream, but she couldn't imagine them after that as she did not know her way home. She had made sure that her father did not say goodbye to her. He did not love her, so there was no need for him to say anything. As far as she was concerned, he preferred losing her to losing her brothers.

In fact, she felt there was no difference between her and the sacrificial hen with a rag tied to its neck. In the rag are roots given to the dead. Sometimes there's a coin in it. That is why you should not pick up any coins you might find lying around, especially at the crossroads. They have the names of murder victims attached to them and if you make the mistake of picking them up and using them, then the dead person will come and haunt your family, until you chase him away with another hen and a coin.

Since she was just another sacrificed bird, she assured herself that she did not need anybody to look after her. The sacrificial animals that one met in the forest—whether poultry, goats or cattle—survived amongst ferocious wild animals, despite having been domesticated. One met the same animal in the same forest season after season. And because her fate did not look very different from theirs, Chinongwa reasoned that the spirits that inhabited these animals and protected them were going to inhabit and protect her as well.

Neither had she wanted her father to say goodbye to her in front of strangers. Yes, they were her family now, but they were still strangers to her, and she did not want to suffer any more embarrassment in front of them. When she had heard her father calling, she had crawled under the hozi and watched people's legs go this way and that while she listened to what they were saying. He must have known she did not want to see him because he did not insist. Instead, he got the cattle from Baba Mashava and the headman, who had already roped them. He conveniently charged Mai Chitsva to say his farewell for him.

Chinongwa had endured Tete Shorai's tearful and profuse hypocrisy and had not felt in any state to suffer her father's. Even though she had promised herself not to shed a tear, her emotions were such that she preferred to brave the separation by hiding under the hozi. Mai Chitsva, who had witnessed her disappearance, looked blank and did not utter a word. Even when her father and aunt left for the cattle pens and Chinongwa crawled out, nobody mentioned that her father had been calling her.

Wangi, the older of the two boys, was silently angry because they had taken his favourite cow, the one that had problems giving birth to its first calf. He had had to pull it out himself. Though the calf had seemed all right, for two days they had feared for Njanji, the cow. Since then, even though it was more than three seasons ago, he felt there was a bond between him and the cow. He knew that Njanji had not forgotten. Did she not have a special look whenever she saw him? Had he not been there to help with the delivery, would the calf, now a heifer, not have died? Even though the heifer had forgotten all about his help and did not seem to give him any special attention, he forgave it and was forever happy to see it jumping around playing the fool. Now this girl with a forever running nose had come and they had taken his Njanji from him. He was sure that the cows in Chinongwa's village, like her, were thin and malnourished and had mucus dripping from their noses and eyes. They were all going to be jealous of Njanji's beautiful shining coat. Tears filled his eyes.

Tawa was the only one who suspected what was going on in his brother's mind for he knew that Njanji was his brother's. Though he did not feel comfortable about the events of the last few days, he also sensed that he didn't fully understand them. But he had long ago learnt that it was safer to accept the world as it was than to try and decipher its intricacies and contradictions. Ever since the death of his mother, whom he no longer remembered, he had tried to look for logic and found chaos. When he had asked for explanations, he had received a slap on the mouth and was told to keep it shut. So that was what he had done. Ironically, this had earned him a reputation as one of the nicest boys in the neighbourhood.

He loved his dog most of all, except maybe for Shamhu. He didn't know whether or not he loved his brother, neither did he crack his head about it. When Wangi was in a bad mood, Tawa knew that the best thing was to avoid him and he left as much distance as possible between them. He would patiently wait for the clearing of Wangi's clouds, as he secretly called them, and was always there when his big brother needed him. Although from time to time, Wangi took his moods out on him, he was the only one to protect Tawa. Often Wangi had come home with a broken nose and bruised ribs from defending his younger brother. And yet he never reproached the young boy for landing him in fights. When their father wanted to know why he'd been fighting, Wangi always explained that it was his fault, not Tawa's.

Although they had to call their stepmother Mai, Wangi did not allow her to punish Tawa, no matter what. Whenever it happened, Wangi would take it out on her at every turn. It was then up to Tawa to shield her from Wangi.

Mai Chitsva knew this, and although she could have told her husband and gained his support, she had decided from the beginning that she was not going to put her husband between her and the children. She was going to win or lose their hearts on her own. She had long ago conceded defeat as far as Wangi was concerned, but she was not going to sell him out.

As long as his father was there, Wangi kept his head low and behaved more or less normally to his 'Mother', but whenever he was not there, the boy went out of his way to punish her, refusing to eat what she cooked, appearing sick so that she had to milk the cows, or disappearing behind the yard and not heeding her calls. When matters were this way, Tawa, feeling guilty and judging the situation unfair to Mai, doubled his efforts and did everything twice as fast or without being asked. When Wangi decided Mai Chitsva had suffered enough, he would become as docile as a lamb.

Tawa knew that today he had better leave some distance between his older brother and himself, though he was not too sure what was going on. At first he had believed what Shamhu had told him about Chinongwa, but after the second day he overheard something that refuted this theory of her being a patient. He could not remember any more what it was. Now 'Mother' had given the father of this girl Wangi's cow.

Mai Chitsva watched the backs of the guests and the cattle with relief and fear. Relief that it was all settled and that the girl was not crying and clinging on to her aunt's skirts, but fear because she was not sure how her husband was going to take the news.

Also she felt disturbed because she did not know Chinongwa's people—where they came from, whether or not they had ngozi or other demons. Now that her people were gone, she was going to put her feelers on the girl and try to find out as much as she could before her husband came home. If it turned out she was possessed, then they would simply return her. But maybe it was too late and the damage had already been done. Maybe she should have asked them to wait for her husband to return before making the decision alone. But then he had already refused them when they had passed the first time. Whatever had possessed her to take such action? Perhaps Musiki had brought the storm and guided the visitors to her house. To think, they had run into the only home in the village where the woman of the house was barren!

Most of all, Mai Chitsva feared her husband was not going to find Chinongwa attractive. If this happened, the girl's people would have to take her back when they came for the rest of the millet. But what about the cattle that she had already given them? If they were as hungry as they had made her understand, they would already have exchanged them for food.

It was when her mind had run like this before the departure of the guests that she had nearly opened her mouth to suggest to the guests that they should wait until her master got back. Only her pride had held her back. They were not to suspect her of weakness.

Had the headman and Baba Mashava, the alcoholic, not come past, the family might have stayed there forever—but they found

111

their feet soon enough. Wangi went to weep in the cattle pen; Tawa, wanting to keep a good distance from his brother, went off with his dog Godo to survey the animal traps; Shamhu disappeared to fetch a larger hari because Mai Chitsva wanted to brew fresh beer for her husband. Mai took her guests into the hut where they ate some of the remaining food from the celebrations.

Chinongwa slinked back under the hozi and fell into such a deep sleep she had to be dragged out after the sun had set.

BOOK 2

1

Amaiguru

The beer that I had brewed to wash down my husband's pleasure in finding a maiden waiting for him was drunk by the village. At first I set a few pots aside for him, but after five days of waiting, I tipped them into the compost at the end of the yard. I understood he had got back from the chief. I waited for him every day, and when there was still no sign of him, I wondered if it was not just rumours. I went to see the person who claimed to have seen him and he assured me he had indeed told him about Chinongwa. I felt unwell. What I had done had not pleased my master. I had brought trouble into my life which, up to then, had been calm waters. How to reverse time or events?

Not only was his not coming home a sign that he was not pleased, but the Marehwas were going to be back any day now to claim the remainder of the cattle and millet. They were going to arrive and the master was not going to be there. What was I going to do? How could I give more of his cattle in his absence? Up to now, I had acted alone, but it was only to please him and make him understand how much I appreciated him, how much he meant to me. I had wanted to show him that I could also be unselfish. I would have given him a maiden from my own people if I could. But I did not want to belittle myself again by returning to my people and asking them for a maiden. I knew that they did not respect me like they did my sisters, who had filled their houses with children. Why would they agree this time when they refused before when I asked for one for my first husband? They would only take pleasure in telling me that it was not possible. As we say, "That which does not belong to you, do not rely on."

Though the danga from my first husband went to my father and, after his death, was inherited by my oldest brother, my oldest brother did not seem in the least responsible for me. Musiki above knew I had to take a complete stranger because I had been refused by my own blood. Even when Baba Chitsva sent another danga for me, they still did not see any reason to turn it back. Of course, they were happy to add the cattle to their huge herds. I was only good for filling their cattle pens.

When I saw these three strangers come into my home, I decided it was Musiki. He knew that my heart was bleeding. Otherwise why, but why should they have come for the second time? I did not do it alone; the whole village was there. Did they not all applaud? And all those men, did they not wish their wives would be as generous? Even all those women who were angry with me, they accepted and recognised my selflessness. It is not every day that we meet with so much generosity.

So the day I heard that my master had been to the village but went away without seeing his new bride, I felt weak. I'm sure my master had reason to go away suddenly, I thought. He can only be pleased with what I have done. We have a respectable herd of cattle. We have a granary near to bursting with all kinds of millet, and our cows produce milk as thick as sadza. He did not need to worry about us going poor or hungry. It can only be that someone knew he was back and took him away for an emergency, somebody whose wife or child was dying. He never refuses anybody, no matter how tired he is.

I found all sorts of excuses for his going away without coming home. It could be when I was at the well or when I went to the river to wash the clothes. Yes, it could only be for an emergency that he had to leave. He would only appreciate what I did for him, so there is no need to worry. What kind of man would not appreciate a young maiden? After a week, Chinongwa already looks different. She has grown cheeks and is filling up nicely. In two or three seasons, she will be ready. I just hope her people will wait until the master comes back. Otherwise I shall have to give them millet only. No more cattle in the absence of the master.

And he was going to accept her, I told myself. And there were going to be babies. I like newborn babies. They are so small, delicate and smell of milk. The home was going to be filled with children, noise and laughter. He was soon going to have as many children as he deserved. I would help look after them. Who knows, they said sometimes it helped open wombs. It could still happen. But I did not want to hope too much just in case I would be disappointed. Because I had been punished and my crime was unforgivable, I knew I was going to pay for it until the day I died.

I appealed to my boy lover as if he were there with me, "I did not want to betray you, but how could I ever explain to my family that I had promised never to love or marry anyone after your death? They would have thought you possessed me, or that your family bewitched me. Forgive me, my loved one! Forgive me and let my womb open! I am imprisoned. I can't tell anybody that I belong to you. They will never understand. I know I committed a grave crime. It is my fault, but have I not paid enough? I was only a child and did not understand it was going to be so difficult to keep my promise. I live in fear every day, waiting for them to discover why I'm barren. Is that not enough?"

As usual, after pleading in vain, my whole body went into spasms that shook me violently from head to toe. I did not fall asleep until the first cock's crow, when I saw my boy lover walking hand in hand with a maiden. I could not see very well if the maiden was me or someone else. Every time I went around to look at her face, she turned the other way, all the time laughing at me.

There was nothing I could do but wait for my master to return. Even if what I'd done had not pleased him, I could no longer change the events. Chinongwa was there and all knew who she was. If only I had kept it quiet and pretended that she was a patient, I could maybe have twisted out of it somehow. Whatever got into me to have that feast without the master?

If only I had seen him before the gossip-mongers had told him what they wanted him to believe. Many never accepted me in the village and were still jealous after all these seasons. They did not think I deserved him and would have preferred to replace me with their ugly daughters. If I had been the first to tell Baba Chitsva about Chinongwa, he would not have gone away before at least taking a look at her.

What gnawed at me most was not knowing what he thought. Even though I tried to reassure myself that all was well, my nights were full of galloping hyenas and spitting cobras standing on the tips of their tails, all laughing and gossiping about how stupid I was, how I was going to suffer for my actions, or that they were going to tie my womb even tighter.

The periods when I lay awake listening to the masters of the night arguing or fighting to be heard were my moments of rest, but sleep did not take long to creep up on me and drag me into the pit of despair. When I fought sleep, I was rewarded with a day that stretched on forever and I could hardly cope with the fatigue that weighed me down by its end. If I did not fight it, I was burdened with nightmares. I did not know which was worse.

118

But I refused to bend down to their laughter. I knew that they were talking about me and were happy at the turn of events, but I denied them the pleasure of seeing me suffering. I kept my head up and dared them to bring me down. During the day, none would have guessed what my nights were like. Even the children—I did not want them to know. During the day, I went to the fields and used the hoe as if my life depended on it. I had to—otherwise I would have fallen into a heap. Because of the storm and the week of rain that followed it, the weeds were growing as if possessed. The maize and millet were choking and beginning to turn yellow. I was fighting against time. Now that we had another mouth to feed, there was no time to be lost. I put Chinongwa together with Shamhu. I did not want her to be alone the first season. I would test her the season after.

The boys knew that something was wrong. I did not realise that they thought Chinongwa was brought in for them until I heard Wangi telling Tawa, who was nearly in tears, that he was going to have to marry her.

2

Chinongwa

Five seasons after my father and Tete Shorai gave me away, I finally went home to see my dying mother. Until then, I had not had any contact with my family. Though I blamed Sekuru for not taking me back to my people, secretly I feared returning. Of course, there were people I missed and would have loved to see again, but returning with my elderly husband was not something I had anticipated. Also, I wanted those who had given me away for food to know that I didn't miss them. While hungrily devouring every bit of news from my village that trickled my way from time to time, I feigned disinterest. But I kept track of who had died or married. When I heard that Ambuya had died, I choked with tears of loss.

By then I had two live children and a third one on the way. My first had died a few weeks after his birth and I still find it hard to talk about him.

I was taken home only because mother was dying, and Sekuru had not given my mother the mombe yeumai, and my father was panicked at the thought of my mother dying without receiving her cow. There had never been masungiro for me, when the m'kuwasha brings one head of cattle, which is slaughtered and fed to the village, and other exceptional guests. And in exchange for another live cow, the bride and her mother step over the daughter's waist beads to thank the mother for protecting her daughter's virginity.

When my father saw my mother sinking, he sent messages that grew more frantic. If mother died without receiving her cow, my father would have had a lot to answer for. Her people, the Taguta clan, would have refused to bury my mother until they received the cow from Sekuru. Back then, I was unaware of the significance of the mombe yeumai or the consequences of it never having been received, but now that I have witnessed scenes where a bloated body can sit for days while the two families wrangle over the payment, I understand my father's insistence on having the ceremony, even when Musiki had opened the door of death. Considering how my father was regarded by my mother's family, and how most of them believed that it was his fault she was dying, I can imagine how much pleasure they would have taken in tearing him apart. They strongly believed that she started wasting away as soon as I was given away, and my having my first child in the 'woods' hastened her descent. So even though my mother could no longer stand or step over my waist beads (her sister did it for her), father insisted masungiro be performed.

It is just as well, because even now I do not see what else would have induced Sekuru to take me home. Amaiguru had given up. I had given up. Still, I think my going back even after five years helped my mother to leave in peace, and my father sighed with relief.

After the cow for masungiro had been killed and consumed, and the mother's cow handed to the Taguta family, everything calmed down. The people left and, for the first time, I found myself alone with my mother. I made sure that my sister-in-law,

Tichafa's wife, who had up to then been looking after my mother, understood I was to be left in charge, and she was only too happy to release her to me.

In the beginning, mother said little, just looked at me. I talked and she smiled, looked worried and sometimes cried. But for me, it was the greatest thing that she or anybody had ever given me. For those hours, I felt loved for the first and the last time in my life. And ever since then, I have known that at least one person has loved me. Moreover, I forgave my mother and felt I understood what she must have gone through when she gave me and my sister up. I decided that one day I would tell my sister that our mother had loved us both, because in the last few days, when her mind was confused, she sometimes called me by my sister's name and when she squeezed my hand it could have been either of us. I shall never know how Muraswa felt about our mother, since I never saw my sister again. She did not come for mother's funeral until after I had left. I keep hoping she understood how much mother had loved us. Or maybe she was able to understand it when she came home to deliver her first baby. She must have had some time alone with mother then, but I shall never know.

Of course, I believed my children loved and needed me. But how does one detach need from love? A child can stick to you simply because you are their whole world. Is that need or love? How is one to know it is not need or fear of losing you?

So, for those two weeks I had with my mother, I experienced maternal love. I immersed my whole self into being with her and I fell in love with her all over again. In times of deep sorrow, I can still think back to those days and awaken that long-ago feeling. And it was love she felt, not need. She did not need me; she knew she was leaving us; Musiki was beckoning to her. Yes, it was clean, untainted love. She had had it for me when I was a child; and in those last weeks, it came flooding back.

123

When I was taken away on the hunt for a husband, I felt betrayed because she had not pulled her hair out and rolled herself in dust in my defence. That then was the kind of love that I would have understood. But now, after all these seasons, after being a mother myself, I finally understood that because we do not protest does not mean we do not love. She had suffered for me. As I looked at her worn face and her eyes sunk in their sockets, I knew she had suffered, even more than I had myself.

Though she did not have enough strength to talk to me, she held my hand and looked and smiled at me. The first time she smiled, I could have choked from the guilt that invaded me. All those horrible, silent accusations I had directed at her. I was convinced that just by looking at me, she could tell what I had thought. How could I look her in the face? But then she kept smiling, and I knew she had forgiven me. She understood and loved me regardless.

At night, I slept on the same reed mat as her, and even though the village women took turns to come and sleep with us every night, in spirit I was alone with her. I slept by the fireside and she was behind me. I felt her mostly hot body against mine when she sweated. I wiped sweat from her forehead with leaves from the mugodo tree to chase away the bad spirits. She would look for my hand in the middle of the night and clasp it in hers. I could tell when the pain was piercing her body, and sometimes I could feel it searing through me. I was happy to share that pain with her; I think she knew she was not alone. Without words, I made her understand that I was going to help her depart as peacefully as possible. That was the only thing that I could do for her. Make her understand that I also loved her, as a mother and a human being.

Every day when the sun was overhead, I bathed her with a cloth and some warm water, into which I crushed the mugodo leaves so as to chase away evil spirits and nightmares. One day, without words, she asked me to wash her hair. I washed it just like one does a baby's who cannot keep its head up. I put her head to dry on my lap. She was happy and smiled and said, "Thank you, my mwanasikana, now I feel clean." Those were her first words in the last three days, for her jaw was more or less clamped shut. They were also her last words to me. I cried. It was the first time that I had not been ashamed of being a girl. I was even proud of it.

Two days later, she passed away. I did not cry. I had cried already, and there were no more tears. I sat and watched her people come and wash and dress her. When they laid her out and her mother's people came to sit over her, I went out to find my children and tell them that their grandmother had gone. I don't remember the words I used, only that my son asked me when she was coming back, and I said, without feeling any pain, "Never. She has gone away to her own people because she was very tired. I think she's going to be happy there. I feel happy for her."

I was thinking of good wonderful Sekuru Taguta, the Fat One, who was the only person from her people whom I had really liked. I could already see him welcoming his sister with open arms.

Part of me envied my mother and wished I had gone with her. Her sufferings were now over. When they beat the drums to announce her death and people from surrounding villages started arriving, wailing, I looked at them in a bemused manner. I felt like chasing some of them away. Hypocrites, rolling themselves in dust! They recovered just as quickly to ask for a piece of meat to roast on the fire. They claimed to be starving.

Since word had gone out that I had finally come for masungiro, there were many who could not wait to have a look at me. I had been gone for five seasons and had two children. For that reason, tongues wagged. People said I had finally come because my mother had said she was not going to die until she saw me and my children. Another version was that she wanted to meet my husband before she died. And yet another ran that she had told my father that if she went away without seeing me and receiving her mother's cow, she would come back and destroy him and his family.

There were those who came to the funeral and were more interested in me than my dead mother. And I was not crying. How could I be sitting there, and outside too, while my mother was inside? I had not seen her for all those seasons and I was never going to see her again. The least I could do was stay in the hut and cry and pull my hair out for her. Many women, after going into the hut and crying over the dead body, and having seen her face, came out. Instead of first going to the men to offer their condolences as is normal, they came to me and, at the sight of me, bawled out all they could. They fell on me. They shook me and smeared their tears on my face, asking me questions to which I did not have answers.

"My daughter, have we now orphaned you? Have we left you alone in the world? Even though you were all alone there, at least you knew you had a mother, my child. Now look at you—all alone! Even though your husband's people did not bring you for your first child, you knew you had a mother. You knew you could come back. A breast that fed you does not reject, it forgives. Even though she has died of heartache, she forgives you!"

I was told all the sins that I had committed. Some told me that had my husband's people brought me to deliver the first child, my mother would still be there, alive and laughing. Had I done this? Had I not done that? How could I have done the other?

I felt suffocated. I had not decided to give myself away. I had not taken myself around, looking for a husband. I had not chosen my husband. My opinion was never called upon. And yet here I was, being accused of having killed my mother. Indirectly, of course, but I could not help feeling that there was general agreement that it was my fault. And somehow I could not help feeling guilty, for was it not true?

I did not know these people any more. I did not belong to them. I was not their daughter, even though they professed to be my mothers, aunts, cousins, uncles, grandparents. I was the younger one who had not come home to give birth to her first child. The older one, Muraswa, was not even there. She was the one with the horrible husband who beat her up for smiling at either animal or man, or for being looked at. Most probably, he did not want her to come to the funeral because there were too many people who might give her ideas about getting a younger man. He most likely was going to come and go back with her when the crowd had gone, after the masadza had been brewed and drunk. By that time, I would be gone too. I kept wondering that had Muraswa been there, would they have accused her as they were accusing me, or was it only me who was guilty?

Five seasons earlier, I had left as a child, a child who was chased outside so that the adults could talk among themselves. Strangely, now, it took me a while to understand that as an adult, I was not going to get into trouble for listening to their conversations. I was no longer eavesdropping.

As it happened, I not only had the right to listen, I was obliged to participate. I was even asked to do so, in spite of not actually wanting to. There was no middle ground. I would have been more than happy to say nothing about myself or my husband.

I would also have preferred to avoid Sarudzai, who was then married to a young man who, she professed, lived for no one but her. Even though some of them had not seen Sekuru, who had stayed for only the two days of masungiro and had not come for my mother's funeral, the word had made the rounds. And the word said that my husband was older than my father and did not love me, and that it was his vahosi who had forced me onto him.

That he had sent a cow to be killed for my mother's funeral somehow relieved me and the situation I found myself in. It offered a few doubts among those who were saying that he did not want me back. Why, after all, would he send a cow for the funeral if he did not care about me at all?

To think that over all those seasons when I was absent, I'd yearned to come home to see these people and visit my favourite places. The well, the fields, the hill, my orchard in the forest, the clay pit and other secret spots. After the burial, all I longed for was to return to my other home. My birth home whose qualities in my imagination had grown with each passing day, no longer existed. Now that I was kumusha and could stay if I chose to, all I wanted was to do was to get away from my people whom I now thought hateful and two-faced.

I longed to be back in the place that I had, until then, never considered home. I could hardly believe that I had longed to return to these now treeless, barren hills, which had once been thick with grass and trees. The area now looked like a woman whose clothes had been stripped off her. She held on to whatever was left, but knew that it was useless. The land was being raped every day: people were multiplying, but the land was not.

In my absence, they had denuded half of my orchard. The shaded rock to which I had always fled when I was unhappy or disconsolate, had been stripped of the vegetation which surrounded it and was now a part of someone else's land. The new owner had cut down the trees that once hid and protected me from prying eyes. And the path to the well now passed through someone else's field, and whenever I made my way there, all eyes followed me: one was afraid even to spit.

My mother, who perhaps had been the only reason to return, had died. My sister, who had never ceased to represent home for me, did not come for my masungiro, even though she had been sent word. It had been a disappointment though not a total surprise. Tete Shorai had manifested some pleasure at seeing me and had played her role as satisfactorily as she could under the circumstances. I realised that I could never really forgive her for begrudging me her husband and blaming me for a situation over which I had no control. To her credit, she did everything to assure the smooth progress of the ceremony, which left me feeling guilty for not acknowledging her.

My father looked more lost than ever. Now that my mother had gone, he did not seem to care for anything any more. His battle was over. I realised how much he had sacrificed for my mother. Was it from love, or guilt? I was certain he had married her for love and had tried to do everything he could to make her life worthy of it—to thank her for loving him? It is hard to know whether or not she loved him. If she didn't, had she ever loved him, and did he know when she stopped doing so? It was clear that, as far as he was concerned, all he had done was mess up her life, and sometimes I wondered if he did not regret having married her. It must be hard to spend one's life trying to make up to someone.

For the first time, all my four brothers appeared to me as much victims as I was. Ngoni, the oldest, had left three seasons ago in search of a bride that he was going to bring back in triumph. But alas! The village was still waiting for that triumphant return and the family was hanging its head in shame. The question now being asked was whether or not Ngoni was going to be brave enough to return at all, even though his hands were empty. While mother was dying, word had been sent to him, but it was uncertain whether he had not returned because he feared that it was a ploy to bring him home to shame him because his hands were empty or because he simply never got the message. For the time being, he was still at a cousin's, a week's walk away. There was no telling when he would hear of mother's death and when or if he would return.

My second brother, Tichafa, in the absence of Ngoni, had married the headman's daughter. The one with the thin leg. She was much older than him. He did not love her, but they already had a child and she was carrying a second. As far as I was concerned, I did not mind her disfigurement. What troubled me was that my brother had to end up marrying a woman older than himself. That said, I must admit that she made up for her deformity with an admirable personality. She did not look down on me because I was married to an old man. She showed me as much respect as

129

she did my brothers. I, in turn, did not show her that I minded her wasted leg or her age. Besides, she was the headman's daughter, which improved Tichafa's standing in the village. And she was as competent as any woman. She could carry a chirongo or firewood the same size as anyone. Her sole shortcoming was that she could not do that with a baby on her back. Her thin leg was shorter than the other and her back was a little bent. When my mother was still alive, she had always looked after the child, but now what would happen?

Dambudzo, my third brother, had left the village when the maiden who had agreed to marry him was given to another man with better prospects. Her father had agreed to the marriage as long as Dambudzo was ready to serve in her family for five seasons, but her mother would not hear of it, neither would she accept the mother's cow from Dambudzo. Not wanting trouble, the good man gave in to his wife and the daughter was married off and left the village. Unable to hold his head high, Dambudzo also left. Nobody knew exactly where he had gone, but some said to work for vasinamabvi in a place called 'Mugodhi', near the end of the world. He would most likely never come back. It was said that the kneeless killed, imprisoned or gave our men magic potions so that they forgot from whence they had come.

All eyes were now on Tafadzwa. He had seen seven and ten summers and become a man in my absence, and I felt some bond with him. Was it the family blood? At first he seemed shy and did not talk much but played with my children. Later, he talked to me about my life, but without judging me or finding me guilty of the death of our mother. He was also a source of information. He knew where everybody had gone and seemed to worry about them. He knew things about my sister and he had been the one Dambudzo had told when he sneaked out of the village. I told him things about me and my life with Amaiguru. He did not ask me questions, but I found myself opening up to him. I still don't know if he loved me or if he listened out of duty. For, besides my mother, I felt nobody loved me, and since I did not love them, I did not feel they owed me anything. But with Tafadzwa, it was like having a friend; I did not feel defensive or threatened. It was like talking to Shamhu. Were brothers supposed to be like that? I did not have an answer. There was no reason why he should have liked me and I did not know what to make of it. I could not bring myself to ask him if he cared for me.

I felt sorry for him because he was going to have to look after father. It was a foregone conclusion that my mother's people would not give my father a chigadzamapfihwa, even though he was younger than my husband. He was not even going to ask. Had they not more or less accused him of having killed my mother even before they went to the n'anga to consult? For the time being, Tichafa's wife was going to cook for father; if Tafadzwa decided to get married, he could use the cattle from my danga.

Even though I had no real daughterly feelings for him, I felt sorry for my father. He had loved my mother and had done his best. The odds were against him from the beginning. Now, since her death, he seemed dead himself, both physically and spiritually. One had the impression he looked without seeing, or he saw only the things that made him tired. His expression did not change whether someone was speaking to him, crying in front of him or laughing. I used to be afraid of him and, when he had left me with Amaiguru, I had loathed him with all the energy that I possessed; but seeing him like this disarmed me. It did not pain me. I just did not hate him any more.

Most of the people in the village had changed too. They had become smaller, bigger, uglier, or older than I remembered them. And then there were those who were no more. They used to be part of my home and suddenly they had gone. Disappeared into the guts of the earth.

I now had to return and confront Amaiguru. As long as I'd been taken there against my will, I had never belonged and had waited for the day when I would return home and refuse to go back to my husband. That had been my plan, my secret that had allowed me to let things pass, pleasant or unpleasant, with as little notice as possible. I wasn't going to let their injustices touch me. Sometimes, I'd even imagined my mother on my side, fighting for me. I now had to take my destiny into my own hands: I would have to return to my jail and fight for my freedom from within.

I stayed a whole week after my mother's burial and was there when her belongings were dispersed. They gave me her hoe and dhuku. Just to say that they had given us something. They were going to keep her old cardigan for my sister. The hoe was worn out and the dhuku and the cardigan both had holes in them. They gave us those token articles so that the rules were followed. If they had had their own way, they would have given us nothing. Many times at a dispersal, I have seen the children being allowed to choose one article each. But if they thought I was going to cry or fight for her belongings they did not know me well. It was they who were fighting. Two of her cousins never spoke to each other again because of the blanket they fought over. It would have killed my mother's heart to see it. It was the gumbeze ramai from Muraswa's husband, the one mother had sworn never to touch as long as her daughter was being mistreated.

When they came to shave my hair off, I did not run away. What did I care? No, I was proud that the whole world should know that I was an orphan; my mother had loved me and I was grieving. Those who ran away were worried about their looks, perhaps because they weren't in pain. So, I was amused when those from my mother's family, who had rolled themselves in ashes to show us how much they were suffering, slunk away when it was announced that the hair shaving was about to begin. My old life ended with the death of my mother; I was happy to start a different one. As my new hair grew, so I felt that I too would grow anew.

Unfortunately, it was the wife of my late and beloved Sekuru Taguta who shaved my head. I never could stand her. She was one of those who had changed from bad to worse. I didn't feel sorry for her even though she had had a raw deal by being inherited by Sekuru Tongai, whom I also detested. It was her fault. If she had chosen one of my uncles to inherit her after the guva ceremony, Sekuru Tongai would never have touched her. She brought it upon herself and ended up with the worst of the eligible husbands she could have chosen from.

I was told that when she was handed her husband's spear to give to her choice of successor among his totem cousins and brothers, that she had handed the spear to her own son. This was a sign that she wanted to remain a widow. It meant that when her son became of age, he would be the head of the family and inherit his father's cattle. Bad calculation. Why she thought people were going to go on fearing her as they used to when Sekuru Taguta was alive, I could never fathom. She will pay for that miscalculation for the rest of her life.

They told me that Sekuru Chenai, a tsvimborume, had cried and begged her to accept him. Sekuru Chenai and Sekuru Taguta had declared themselves *alter ego* brothers long before Sekuru Taguta had got married. Each would inherit the other's wife in case of death. That was why Sekuru Chenai was so sure of his chances. Still, a little bit drunk from the all-night guva ceremony, he had gone round the huts crying, "Have you refused four legs under the blanket, my beauty? How can you lay to waste those thighs, my *alter ego's* wife? And those round buttocks? And those breasts ...? All gone to waste at your age. You're going to have only two legs under the blanket like me with my miserable two legs under my blanket. Let's unite together, my dear. When we were growing up, your husband and I promised to look after each other's wives if one of us died young. Don't you have any respect for an old promise between brothers?"

All this, to the ululations of Sekuru Taguta's family women and applause from the men folk. But his widow had stayed firm.

Two days after the ceremony, Sekuru Tongai, with alcohol cruising once more in his veins, broke her door down in the middle of the night and claimed her in not so discreet a manner. In the morning, while she stayed inside out of shame, Sekuru Tongai was seen fixing the door as if, all along, he had been meaning to do so. That was how she became his third wife and how Sekuru Tongai inherited the cattle of Sekuru Taguta, as well as his land and children. Though the village did not approve of the method, there was a sigh of relief that there were to be no young widows walking around and tempting the men. Because people felt she had always carried herself a few rungs higher than she should have, there was little sympathy for her.

Now, seeing her again, she did not look as proud as she used to. Now she was just one of three wives, and her children from her first husband were not her second husband's favourites. If she wanted her children to have what belonged to them, she had to sacrifice her pride and accept her new lowly status as an inherited wife. If she had chosen Sekuru Chenai, the tsvimborume, at least she would not have had co-wives.

The other two wives ganged up on her because of how she had looked down on them before her husband died. Her wounded vanity had since transformed her into an old, bitter rag. It made me feel guilty to know that I did not feel at all endeared to her. When she finished shaving my hair, I gave her a penny, which I knew she desperately needed.

So this was my home and I was not going to regret leaving it once more. The only thing I was happy to take with me was my mother's love. This I secretly tied inside her old dhuku. Whenever I felt unloved, unwanted or rejected, I would take that dhuku and put my head in it and feel my mother's love once more. It would keep me strong.

I was more than glad when Tete Shorai gave excuses for not taking me back, "You know I have to be here for all those who are coming to offer their condolences. I have been charged with taking them to her people and I have to help Tichafa's wife with the cooking. Your father, poor man, is in no condition to do anything. I therefore say goodbye to you, my child, and I shall come and see you as soon as I can. Console yourself, my dear."

"Thank you. I shall be waiting for you. It is impossible for you to leave now, but console yourself."

"I'm glad you understand, my father's one. But tell Baba Chitsva and Amaiguru that I shall be there before the first rains."

Even though we both knew we were lying to each other, it was more comfortable that way. Tafadzwa, in the role of my father, accompanied me back to my betrothed.

3

Amaiguru

When he came back from Bikita and saw her for the first time, he swore he would never touch 'that creature'. This was after three weeks of fattening her up. When her people had returned for the remainder of the cattle and grain, I had given them millet from my own granary, not his, telling them the cattle would follow when the master came back. So when Baba Chitsva told me to go and fetch his cattle back from her people, I didn't know what to do—or where to go. I had not expected events to turn this way. I was not going to go to her people—I, a woman—and claim his cattle. What were they going to think?

Instead, I left for two weeks and visited my own people to tell them what had happened. It was because they blamed me that, for the first time, I poured out what had been troubling me. I told my brothers and their wives, "If, when I had asked you for a maiden for my first husband, you had given me one, do you think he would have taken another wife? No, his people would not have forced another woman on him. And I would not have run away from him.

137

Because you, my family, refused to give me one of my nieces so that I could offer her to my husband to have children for both herself and me, I had no choice but to leave."

My brothers looked at each other, not daring to answer me. When the silence got too long, the oldest brother, not looking at me but his wife, threw the blame back at me. "Instead of running to Chitsva, if you had come here and asked for a niece, we would have obliged. We did not know that you had run away until your ex-husband came here looking for you, and we did not know where you were."

He was trying to put a web over my eyes by pretending they would have given me a niece for my first husband. I was not to be fooled. "It is too late now, and all I came here to tell you is that, because of your selfishness, I have had to take a complete stranger and offer her to him—him who has made me a woman again. And now listen to me, all of you. When I die, let me be buried like a dog, for I am but a dog, and there is no guva ceremony for a dog. I do not want to see you at my funeral. You took the cattle from my first husband when father died, and you took the cattle from Chitsva but did nothing for me in return. If you show your heads at my funeral, I shall let my shadow climb the wall and everybody will know. So on you all, I spit and shit!"

They and their wives all started protesting at once.

"If Chitsva wants a wife from us," one of them said, "why does he not ask himself? If he makes the demand, we shall think about it."

I stood up, took the bast that I had kept on my head under my dhuku, and I broke it in two before they could realise what was happening. I threw the other piece at my oldest brother who tried to pull me back inside the hut in order to tie the two pieces back before I could get out, but it was too late. I ran out and our ties were broken.

138

As I walked away from them, my oldest brother's voice was chasing me, "Don't you ever come back here, or I shall chop your head off! No wonder you have no children! No wonder your womb does not open! You have winds possessing you to dare come here to break ties."

When I looked back, my two younger brothers were pinning him to the ground. The axe with which he had wanted to cut my head off was lying next to him. The women were wailing while trying to pull the brothers apart. There was a cloud of dust around them.

Feeling better for having relieved my chest, I left for one of my sisters and stayed there for more than a week while the tempers cooled on the Chitsva side. When I finally went back home, things seemed indeed to have cooled down. The subject of discord was no more alluded to and we pretended that all had been well when I left. I looked after Chinongwa as if she was my own child. I defended her and myself from those who dared insinuate that she was a bad seed by making allusions to the poorest ever harvest that followed her arrival. I did not heed the advice of those who thought Chinongwa should be given to the boys instead of their father. "I took her for Baba Chitsva," I kept saying, "and now she belongs to him."

I know there were some who celebrated when Baba Chitsva said he wanted nothing to do with a little girl. They wished the situation to deteriorate, but to their disappointment it did not. When I came back from my people, the headman had spoken to Baba Chitsva and either he decided to accept her or he did not want to make any more allusions to something that had already caused such disharmony.

The two seasons that followed were quiet and our lives went back to normal. Though the boys did not accept her, there were no major problems. Chinongwa and Shamhu got on well. Though Chinongwa was never going to attain that stature that made a woman stand out among others, she could hold her own. Yes, the mucus made the bad habit of coming back every once in a while, but I had taught her to wash her face three times a day, and when she did not forget one hardly noticed her eyes.

Her speech came back one moon after I returned from my people. One day I said to Baba Chitsva, "Why don't you do something about the child's deafness?" I always referred to her as 'the child' so as not to wake the sleeping demons in him.

"She's not deaf. She's not dumb. She just has an uninvited visitor who has taken abode in her being."

"Is the person stronger than you?"

I'd thrown him a challenge. How could anybody be stronger than him?

That very evening when he came back, I could smell the mixture he had concocted. Before sunrise the following morning, I woke her up and brought her to the door. He hid himself beside the door so that anyone coming inside the hut would not see him, his left hand holding the calabash with the mixture and his right holding the bushy tail, to be dipped into the mixture. I pushed her in front of me and stood in the doorway so she could not run out. As soon as she entered, Baba Chitsva splashed her right in the face with the tail. He chanted, "Whoever you are, get out of her. Go and find somewhere else to make your home. It is I of the Shava totem, and I am stronger than you. I order you to get out and leave this cave. Now! I of the Shava totem hereby declare war on you. Man or woman, I challenge you to a fight here and now. If you are a man, show me your balls; I shall show you mine. If you are a woman, show me your breasts; I shall show you mine."

All the while, he was splashing the smelly liquid in Chinongwa's face with all his vigour. At first, she hid her face until the smell became unbearable and she started howling. But Baba Chitsva doubled his efforts. "I shall not leave until you talk. Declare yourself, coward, declare yourself!"

140

After what seemed an eternity, with sudden violence and without warning, she spoke in a man's voice, "I'm not going. You are no match for me. Leave me alone or I shall break you. If you knew whom you were dealing with, you'd be trembling."

Baba Chitsva was not to be intimidated. Even though he was not sure if the other was stronger or bluffing, he raised his voice higher. "We shall see. I've never lost! I warn you, beware of playing with me!"

Baba Chitsva began roaring like a lion; jumping and splashing even more violently. With every splash, Baba Chitsva groaned as if he was in pain. Chinongwa did not stop struggling and I was sweating and getting tired. It was as if I was struggling with an adult. Then, suddenly, she was a bellowing bull; her body went stiff. With Baba Chitsva roaring and Chinongwa bellowing, the noise was too much.

"Stop splashing me. Who do you think you are? You do not know who I am. You're playing with fire. I have warned you!"

Without warning, she lunged out at Baba Chitsva, pulling me down with her. We both fell just outside the hut, me over her.

"Pin her down! Do not get up!" Baba Chitsva howled.

I stayed put but twisted my face around so I wouldn't get splashed. Then I heard a voice from under me, "It smells in here. Let me go! I can't take it any longer. But where do I go? I was well in there. Oh no, let me go! It stinks in here, oh how it stinks. Let me out of here, please, let me out!"

Baba Chitsva, sensing victory, was jumping up and down, thundering and splashing. Feeling her body loosening, I got off her. She tried to get up but fell down into a small heap in front of the door, holding onto her stomach. She turned round and round on her left side like a dog that has been bitten by a snake. There was agony in her face and she moaned and wailed. Baba Chitsva kept assailing her until she stopped moving and her voice subsided. I picked her up like a bundle and carried her into the cooking hut where a fire was burning, then I put her on the mat and covered her with a blanket. She slept the whole day and never remembered anything about this episode afterwards.

We never found out who the uninvited visitor into her being was because he never declared his name. We only knew from the voice that it was a man. In less than a week, she was speaking just like anybody else. After that, I started on her, as she was lacking in everything womanly. Yes, she was polite, and yes, she worked hard, but the way she sat, the way she walked! And yet her tete was as well-bred as could be. I did not understand. It was going to be a long way to go, but I was determined. I knew how to turn a girl into a woman. Luckily, I had just begun seriously with Shamhu and I made the two of them do everything together. I did not want Baba Chitsva to have any excuses. And those people in the village, I was going to confound them all.

Up to then, Baba Chitsva hardly looked at her, but I was going to change all that. I gave myself two seasons. Even if she was not yet washing, two seasons from then was going to be enough. Her education would have been done and, in cases like this, one should always strike while the iron is hot. Baba Chitsva had to come to her mat at the earliest possible moment. At the rate I was feeding her, she could only grow. By the end of her first moon, she was eating like that cow from grassless pastures.

But every day I had to repeat that she should sit properly, cross her legs, show nothing to the public, walk like a woman and not thrust her head forward like a gossip-monger. It was a big struggle to make her walk a bit more slowly, in a dignified manner, instead of running like one being chased by a hundred demons. Whenever she laughed, she forgot herself. When she heard the boys whistle, she also whistled. She wanted to climb trees. Imagine a woman who climbs trees! Whatever her age, she was already a married woman and I had to be careful. Her tete had left her in my hands. I did not want the other girls to influence her in any way. The smaller girls

I did not mind, but the bigger ones were already thinking of other things. While it was harmless for Shamhu, if not beneficial, I was not too sure of the effect on Chinongwa. She did not like it when I told her she could not always go to play with Shamhu and her friends; I do not think she understood. But how does one explain anything like that to a child her age?

The worst was the second mahumbwe. I let her go to the first one because she had just arrived. It was only four moons after her arrival and she did not know many people in the village. In any case, a game for 'playing houses' was not completely useless. So I let her go with Shamhu and the two boys, and they cooked with the children from the headman. She played one of the children. Shamhu played the mother and the father was one of the sons of the headman. They all went into the fields to get the leftovers from the harvest. I gave them what I could, and that week we went twice to eat with them. It was not bad and Chinongwa said that the following year she would like to play mother and have her own children, like Shamhu. It was not wise just then to tell her that the following year she was not even going to go to mahumbwe.

Maybe I should have let her go. It is unlikely that anything would have happened because everybody knew that she was betrothed by then. But I could not risk it. Every day I feared. What is the use of leaving traps around and saying the mouse is going to be careful? So she did not participate in the second mahumbwe, but came with me to the cooking site to test the food, just like the other adults.

On her second year with us, the children were told not to call her by her first name any more. The boys, though resenting this at first, were to call her Mainini; Shamhu was to call her Ambuya, like she called me. After all, they had to give her the respect that her position demanded, and the earlier the better. She continued to call Baba Chitsva Sekuru, but then she had always copied what Shamhu did. I did not ask her to change it and I do not know what she would have called him anyway. With all those guests coming and going, there would have been some explaining to do.

How I fought with Baba Chitsva to make her go and see her mother before she died! All those seasons when he didn't want to go for masungiro, I did everything I could; I threatened, grovelled, cried. Had it not been for me, she would never have seen her mother before her death. When after five seasons they sent the messenger to say her mother would not last long and that they should bring her daughter, I told Chinongwa to cry until Baba Chitsva changed his mind. I asked the messenger not to leave without him.

The messenger, bless his heart, stayed, and on the third day Baba Chitsva gave in and went to the cattle pen with the headman to select seven head. The mother's cow, the ox to be killed for masungiro, and the other five to complete the three that had been taken initially. Not many people nowadays have so many cows paid out for them. Even for me he did not pay as much. Just five head. Yes, I have not had any children, but that is not my fault, and apart from that there is nothing that anyone can reproach me for. Still, her parents, thanks to me, received more cows for their daughter that they gave away than many other parents do.

Because he had taken so many seasons to bring their daughter to her family, I thought it would be a good idea if the herd was big. They would be impressed enough to forgive him. But when he went to talk to the headman, it was suddenly all his idea. The headman came back to tell me how lucky I was to have such a man for a husband.

"I went down on my knees, Mai, and I bent my head and clapped my hands to him, because, Mai, there are not many men like him. I myself am far, very far away, from a man like that. It is a pity, Mai, that in this pitiful world of ours, most of us are more interested in what we can get than what we can give. He's a good man, Mai. I can assure you from deep down in my heart that I have respect for a man like that. Keep him away from the fire. We need him in this world, even as an example to humble others."

When he came back just after masungiro, my husband had grown in size. He could barely fit into his clothes any more. He could only look down on us little mice. All the cajoling, threatening, crying and whining that Chinongwa and I had gone through to make him go to the ceremony were forgotten. When the messenger came to announce that her mother had passed away, he flew to the wetlands where the cows were grazing to select a fat ox for the funeral of his precious newfound mother-in-law. I wasn't even consulted. He didn't go himself, however, but sent one of his cousins to represent him. He said he had a special patient who needed care at that moment.

I was going to ask him to go after the patient had left, but I said to myself, "What are you getting out of this, my Maidei? Who is going to thank you?" I spoke to myself using my own name, my maiden name; I spoke to the person I once was.

So I did not suggest anything and he never went. What a shame. I wonder what they think of it. Her father must have waited and waited for him to come.

Then Chinongwa came back with her younger brother, and Baba Chitsva was not even ashamed to offer him his condolences here in his own home. Luckily, the brother was only a child and could not refuse his hand. I would have refused it.

But it was after the brother returned that the circus began.

As soon as she came back from the funeral, I knew something had happened. Maybe she had always had demons within her that all along she had subdued, I couldn't tell. Or perhaps her family had given her some bitter roots when she went to mourn her mother. Maybe she told them she did not like to live with a vahosi, and they told her to get rid of me.

Remember that I had done everything I could to help her and her family. I took it upon myself to feed and educate her, to be her mother, father, tete and family. To wipe her tears, her arse. And during the scabies epidemic, I washed her sores and squeezed the pus out. Was she my blood? I raised a dog on milk thinking that tomorrow it was going to remember and thank me. Guess what I got? Bites. Dog bites from a rabid animal that has a memory shorter than a fly's—one that leaves a fraction of its brains every time it shits. Yes, that is the thanks I got!

When she started to turn against me, I thought that he, who had always been the centre of my life, was going to right everything, as he had always done. But this time he was not there. He turned his face from me and stood on her side. And yet, he had always sworn that he did not love her.

I had given her her own cooking hut after the birth of her second child, but she used it to sleep in. Most of the time, she used my hut to do her cooking. Even when she used hers, she always brought the food to my hut and we would all eat together.

I did not ask her to bring the food to my hut, as she later accused me. Even the first week when I gave her a hut and she did most of the cooking there, she always came to eat with us. After a week, she decided she didn't want to have her own hut and do the cooking by herself and eat alone. I suggested that maybe Baba Chitsva would take turns to eat with me and then her, but she did not want that. He himself did not care what we did. He did not seem in the least interested and did not give us any house rules, so we did what we wanted. As long as he was fed, he did not care who had done the cooking.

Since she has been back, I stand accused of giving her a hut as if I was her mother-in-law. But we did not have a mother-in-law. It was advice that I got from the headman's wife, and I fully agreed with her. If things had been normal and we had a mother-in-law, it would have been her duty to give her a cooking hut after the apprenticeship period of a season or two. If I had not given her

146

a hut, I would have been accused of treating her like a child and exploiting her.

On giving her the hut, I invited the whole village, killed my own chicken that Baba Chitsva did not pay me for, and I gave her a granary with everything from peanuts to rapoko. I went to the potter to buy her pottery, but she brought it all into my hut to be used. Normally, if Baba Chitsva had taken her for masungiro, her own people would have bought her all that when they brought her back, but I had to be her mother, tete and mother-in-law all in one. It was I who went to see the headman so that he gave her a plot of land. Baba Chitsva did not want to give her part of his, even though he never cultivated it all. He said he did not want to have a woman near him. So the headman gave her a plot next to mine so that I could help her with the children.

The first seasons were not easy for her. She was still a child. So when I finished hoeing the first weeds in my plot, I went in to help her. How many times did I find her fast asleep when everyone else was working? Whenever the baby cried and she went to feed him in the shade of the tree and to make him take his nap, she fell asleep with the baby, and at times it was hard to know who the mother was and who the baby, for the baby would wake up first. I never breathed a word of this to Baba Chitsva or the people in the village. How many women have been beaten up because they were caught sleeping instead of weeding? But I just continued my education and hoped she was going to become more responsible and give in less to the demands of the flesh. If only I had known. Just the weeds in her plot would have told the world who she really was.

I should have been warned when she went behind my back to ask him for clothes. If she had told me that she wanted her own dresses, I would have told Baba Chitsva. Whenever she wanted to go out, to the stores or anywhere, I always lent her my going-out dress. I even gave her permission to borrow it when I was not there so that she did not have to wait for me. When we needed salt, it was usually she who went to the stores with the other women. I wanted her to be independent. So most of the things that I used to do I let her do so that she would not be lost without me. Now I am being accused of making her my servant and giving her orders.

Where she used to tell me where she was going, she now slinks away like a thief. She went to the potter to order more pottery and then she went to order a mortar and pestle—all behind my back. I did not ask any questions and I looked aside when she thought that she was slipping away. She said things about me. But what she said came back to me. And she started making friends with some people with questionable reputations. To all that I said nothing, I only watched.

When I asked Baba Chitsva what was happening, he said he did not want to know and did not care about women's affairs. But the question that I asked myself was that if he did not care as much as he said, why was he paying for her behind my back? It was only when I asked him that he said he did not want to know. When she asked him for new things, he paid and did not say it was women's affairs. Now that his children were grown because I had wiped their arses, and he had a young wife, he did not need me any more and what I said did not count. I felt I was the stranger and she the one who belonged.

4

Chinongwa

When my people left me with Amaiguru, her immediate concern was to fill me up and ensure I seduced her husband. "A desirable woman must have legs that are worth talking about, buttocks that shiver when she walks, a calf to fill a man's palm, and breasts as large as paw-paws and as firm as mangoes."

Her plan to achieve this was simply food: food and more food. She fed me day and night. And she did not forget to take me to the elephant tree, underneath which I had to sing for the kind of breasts she wished me to have for Sekuru to fondle.

So I ate and ate. "In less than two weeks," she told me later, "you started to fill out and your skin began to glow. You cast off your old skin like a snake. You became a new person, so new that when your brothers returned two weeks later to get more millet, they did not recognise you. You grew into a woman in a single season."

What she ignored was how fast I grew inside. I crossed thresholds at lightning speeds. When I arrived, I was just a child from a hungry home who had left her mother and father behind. I was, yes, but my mother had protected me from the harsh world as much as she could. I was not ready for the adult world, with its hypocrisy, innuendo, lies, half-truths and brutal facts. I did not know how to assess and respond to words that did not mean what was said.

Amaiguru made me cross all the obligatory rivers and mountains in the little time she had and I grew from being a child into a young woman, a desirable bride, a wife, a mother and a stepmother, in just two seasons. According to Amaiguru, one day I was a child and the next an adult. Though I was a child in body and mind, I was also, like her, a married woman. "You cannot go out and play as if you were a normal child. What if something happened to you? How could I ever face Baba Chitsva? How could I explain it? I gave my word to your Tete Shorai that I would look after you and I'm not going to be found wanting. You stay here with me and I shall show you how to brew cooking soda. We're running out of it and it needs to sit for a few days before it is ready. Don't compare yourself with Shamhu."

So I watched longingly as Shamhu went off to play while I stayed home and learnt to be a seductive woman and a mother to Wangi, Tawa and Shamhu. But sometimes, seemingly arbitrarily, she decided that I could be a child. "Go and play with Shamhu and the other girls. Stay as long as you want, as long as the two of you don't whistle or climb trees."

Shamhu and I would watch longingly while the boys climbed the trees, whistled as they went about their chores, or sat at the dare with the men to hear the latest village quarrel. When we went into the woods to gather firewood, we would whistle to our hearts content, though we were always on the look out for those adults who enjoyed telling tales. But the main thing that we were not allowed to do and were most envious of doing was going to school. Wangi and Tawa went. And not only were we to do their chores when they were not there, but we had to watch while they learnt to read and write. Although we were only half convinced that their scratches meant anything, we were still jealous and resentful. Sekuru was not interested in school and would have forbidden the whole enterprise if Amaiguru had not thought it important (one of her brothers was a teacher). Nonetheless, the boys did not go to school every day; they went less when Sekuru was at home and more often when he was not.

During the rainy season, they went even less because there was weeding to be done and cattle to be looked after. At times, the rivers were flooded and they could not get to school anyway. Amaiguru made them take turns so that one boy was always available to look after the cattle because Sekuru held education in contempt, "Who has ever seen anybody bringing food from school, no matter how much time they spend there? What do you harvest at the end of the year? Have the boys not always come back with empty hands? Who has ever eaten reading and writing? Can you put them on a plate to serve the hungry? Is it not just another vasinamabvi trick to turn our children away from us? Do you want our sons to become albinos with no knees?"

But Amaiguru was adamant that the boys should continue with their schooling and would sometimes ask Tawa to write something on the slate for her and she would admire it with a big smile on her face.

Other intimate womanly secrets united Shamhu and me. We both had to sit with our legs crossed so that none could see the flowers between our legs. We had to pull the little 'ears' down there between our legs every evening so that they became as long as Amaiguru's middle finger.

"If those ears are not long enough, your future husbands will send you back and claim back all they paid for you. Do you know what shame will befall me, on the whole family and village?"

Amaiguru inspected their lengths from time to time. We were relieved when she let us stop when they got as long as her little finger.

We also had to make sure we kept ourselves virgins so that the husband got what he paid for with his cows. "Any maiden who has been pierced before marriage will, on the first night, be discovered. The morning after, the tete of the shamed husband will bring the bride back to her family, together with an egg whose contents had been emptied through a small hole. The shame that will befall the family is beyond description and that family will never again hold their heads up. I've seen mothers of brides commit suicide. I've seen them chased back to where they came from. I've seen shamed families leave their village having to start again where nobody knows about their shameful past."

Even in the faraway village, matters like this are whispered from one to the other and heads are shaken. Then questions are asked, "But who has committed such a crime?"

The maiden had to watch out for that man who dared to attempt touching someone's goods, and she always had to report it. At times, blood flew because of such things—and there were even cases of young girls killing themselves if nobody else from the clan reached them first. These tales sent chills down our spines, and we pulled harder on those little ears and kept our legs crossed tightly to protect our virginity and avoid bloodshed.

Men were hyenas, we were goats; they would make one mouthful of us. So in their presence, and to avoid being gobbled, we were not to laugh too loudly, not to have direct eye contact and, most important of all, we were to keep our legs crossed at all times to protect that which was in between.

As a sign of respect that would make us desirable wives, we were also to go down on our knees when serving men. We were to ask how they were before they could ask us, and we were to curtsy when greeting them. We practiced walking slowly and swinging our bottoms like well-bred women who were not being driven by evil spirits. We also learned to clap our hands in a womanly manner and say thank you for anything we received. And no matter how small the object was, it was to be received with both hands because nothing was ever too small. Everything, regardless of size, was too big for us; we did not deserve it and should be grateful even to be offered it.

All this was going to assure us a good standing in society and we were going to be admired wherever we went. Men were going to so desire us that by the time we came of age, I imagined a long queue of them waiting patiently to be chosen by us—maidens with long ears between their legs. Our parents could then charge as much roora as they wished for; they would know that we were not going to be brought back for any reason whatsoever.

My tragedy was that I was never going to be free to marry a man in the normal way, in spite of the effort I was making. Did I not already have my husband? Many times I felt jealous of Shamhu, who was going to have all those men desiring her while I was stuck with her uncle. I was working for nothing. I was not going to reap any rewards for having little ears as long as Amaiguru's middle finger. The man I was working for did not even desire me. Everybody knew he did not desire me because he said it as loudly as he could. That was why I wasn't sent home for masungiro when the time finally arrived. Sekuru Chitsva—I called him Sekuru because that was what he was to Shamhu—did not want to meet my family. As far as he was concerned, a man of five tens and more seasons presenting himself as the husband of a baby with milk on her nose was nothing but ridiculous. What were they all going to think of him?

So when my first child was due to come not long afterwards, instead of returning to my family as was the custom, Sekuru said I would have to have it at the Chitsva home, with Amaiguru giving me the dilation medicine that my mother should have given me.

I'd been told that even my sister, with a husband like hers, had come home for her first child. My mother had stepped over my sister's waist beads and received her cow. Of course, my sister was not allowed to stay the usual moon after having the baby, but went back 'bleeding', as my mother said.

Amaiguru tried everything she could to make Sekuru agree to send me home for the ceremony, but he wouldn't hear of it. He told her that since she'd decided to be the man of the house and marry for him, she could go ahead and finish what she'd started. I don't think Amaiguru believed him at first. She thought he would surely change his mind. When she realised that he would not do so, she sent for the headman and his wife to talk to him. The result was that he beat her up for the first time. The next morning when we woke up, he'd disappeared and we did not know where he was. I washed her swollen face with warm water and both of us cried. I remember that day, wishing she were my mother.

So while sending prayers to the Chitsva totems, the Marehwa totems and her own totems, Amaiguru started to go around the villages to look for a midwife for me. This was a difficult task because nobody wanted to touch me. "What if something went wrong?" people asked. If my family was not there, they would think that any problems were the fault of the midwife. Finally, only the toothless midwife accepted, and Amaiguru had to swear to take full responsibility for any problems that might occur in front of the headman and his wife.

Three moons from the birth of my first child, Amaiguru took me away from Sekuru's mat and she went back to sleep with him. I went back to sleep with Shamhu, who was to call Amaiguru when the pains started.

Although she would not have admitted it to anyone, I knew Amaiguru was constantly regretting having taken me for Sekuru. To begin with, Sekuru had known before he got back from treating the chief's wife that he had a bride-in-waiting. He was told that she was nothing but a skeleton, that she was deaf and dumb, and that she might have ngozi. He also learned that his wife had already given three head of his cattle to the in-laws, who would be coming back for more millet in two weeks. As she soon realised, none of this would have made him especially pleased with Amaiguru.

On hearing all this, Baba Chitsva had turned away and walked for five days to go to Bikita, where his brother and the rest of the Chitsva clan lived. We never found out exactly what Sekuru Chitsva's brother told him, but we understood that Sekuru's brother was happy that Amaiguru had gone out of her way to find a bride for Sekuru. He couldn't understand why his younger brother did not appreciate what his wife had done for him. We also understood that Sekuru Chitsva returned home because his older brother had hit his wife after they had quarrelled about me. Sekuru Chitsva's sister-in-law had agreed with him that he should not take a child for a wife, and added that only selfish old men would do that, and this put her husband into a rage, assuming that he was the old man being alluded to. When Sekuru Chitsva tried to intervene, the whole affair blew up in his face, with both husband and wife blaming him for their fight. While the neighbours tore the husband from the wife, Sekuru Chitsva took his hat, walking axe and spear, and, his tail between his legs, he came back home.

Because of that fight, the two brothers never talked to each other again. For the rest of his life, Sekuru would never stop reproaching me for dividing his blood.

5

Chinongwa

After Tafadzwa left, I decided to return to my own hut. I no longer had a home. I had to build my nest here. No longer a child, there was no other choice but to be a mother to my two children, and with a third on the way. I decided that the first thing to do was to refuse to be ordered around by Amaiguru and to become an adult.

She was no longer to tell me when to wake up, where to sleep, what to eat. I was going to ask Sekuru for money to buy dresses. No more borrowing them from Amaiguru. I would go to the store by myself, choose the cloth I liked and get the tailor to measure and make it for me. No more accepting her hand-me-downs which always needed mending. No more cast-offs that were too big for me. Were we not both the wives of Sekuru Chitsva? My children would have clothes made from my old dresses, not hers. Let her eat her own cast-offs.

She had completely forgotten that I had the same rights as she did—or had she really? I respected that she was the vahosi, but that was all. She was not my husband. The only person that I should obey was him. After all, the other vahosi in the village did not dictate to their younger wives. They respected them as they did their own younger sisters. Why then did Amaiguru not respect me?

I was finished with washing her clothes. When I went to the river, I would not tell anybody; I would take my own and my children's clothes and disappear quietly. And I would have two everyday dresses just as she did, so that when one was being washed, I could wear the other, instead of waiting at the river for it to dry. I would refuse to be teased because I always sat almost naked waiting for my dress to dry. You would not think that my husband was a n'anga.

And when there was a gathering to which everybody was invited, I would no longer wait for Amaiguru to come back and lend me our going-out dress before I could take my turn. She would never let me go first. I know she often stayed so long so that there would be nobody left when I finally arrived at the party, but she always pretended to hurry and quickly take off our dress, "Here, here, off you go before everybody is gone."

In the end, I would tell her that it was not necessary to go after all. She knew exactly what she was doing. And not only did she return late, but she sat and told me how wonderful it had been. Was that not to fill me with envy? Now, all this was over. I would do as I pleased.

My first chore was to clean my cooking hut and put everything in place. From now on, I would cook and eat there every day. I would ask Sekuru to build me another hut to sleep in.

There were many things that I would have to do if I was not to be dependent on her. I did not have much to my name. I would have to have my own grinding stones: one for millet and another for peanuts. I also needed my own mortar and pestle.

Everybody in the village agreed that she did not respect me as much as I deserved. Some advised me never to be too dependent

158

on my vahosi. But since my plan had always been to return to my people, I'd listened to them with a knowing smile feeling that my situation was only temporary. I would go away never to return to this accursed village. I would have the last laugh.

While Shamhu was with us, Amaiguru treated us both like children. But when Shamhu went away to be married, she still treated me like a child, and although she called Shamhu Mai va Chipeneti, because her first child's name was Chipeneti. In the village, they all called me Mai va Tinashe because I had two children, but to her I was still Chinongwa—and she called me thus in front of everybody. Even complete strangers suffered my humiliation.

But all this was in my mind, and when I came back full of determination, I moved it slowly to give Amaiguru enough warning that things would never be the same. First, I waited for Tafadzwa to return. Even though he did not say anything, he must have noticed how I was being treated; one had to be blind not to see it. In any case, even if he had wanted to lodge a complaint, Tafadzwa could not have said anything to the wall, for Sekuru went away soon after we arrived and did not come back until my brother had left. How could Tafadzwa speak to Amaiguru about not treating me like a married woman? She was not my husband.

When Sekuru came back, I asked him to order me my own mortar and pestle and grinding stones. I was afraid he was going to ask me why I needed them when Amaiguru had some, but he did not ask any questions. That was a relief because I don't know how I would have explained it. I am almost sure that if he had questioned me, it would have been the end of my projects. I had never been able to speak to him. Whenever I had wanted anything, it was always Amaiguru who spoke for me. I was not always there when she did so. When Amaiguru and I suspected that Sekuru was not going to be too eager to produce what we wanted, Amaiguru always told me she needed to work on him first. As a result, I had been shy to ask for anything. I didn't know how to 'work on him'. Asking for the stones was the first time I ever asked my husband for anything.

As to the potter, I did not need Sekuru because I took my own rapoko in exchange for all the cooking pots and serving bowls that I needed. Pots are a woman's affair anyway.

Sekuru had asked the thatcher to start on my sleeping hut, so early every morning, before sunrise, I would go to cut grass for the roof. Because I did not want to ask Amaiguru for anything any more, I could get only one bundle of thatch grass a day. I couldn't go for a second one on the same day because the children would be up. It took me more than two weeks to cut enough to thatch the roof of the hut. Already they had started the wall. I did not want them to have to wait for me so the bundles that I brought were big and heavy. But I was determined because Amaiguru had always said I was not capable of doing anything by myself and that she always had to be behind me. This time I was going to make everyone see that I was quite capable of looking after myself. I was not going to ask her for one single thing. Not even embers to start a fire. Every night before sleeping, I would make a heap of all the cinders, so that in the morning I would be able to blow some fire out of them. I had to be very careful. Amaiguru would have loved to see me fail. I owed it to my mother, who I now knew had loved me, and I owed it to my children, who had nobody but me.

Amaiguru started to look at me askance when she saw me so busy, but I acted as if nothing was new. I had sworn to myself I was never going to be mean to her. All I wanted was my independence. Nobody would wake me up one day, and give me my independence on a plate! But my actions and capability did not please my mentor. She had always told everybody that whatever she put in my head in the morning had gone by the afternoon, so she was obliged to refill it the next day. The thought that I had a brain capable of of logic or of disentangling a rope was too much for her.

So Amaiguru started a rumour that I was plotting against her, that there were people in the village who were influencing me, people with misguided intentions. If anybody did as much as talk or laugh with me, she barred them from her list of friends. In no time, the village was divided into those who talked to me and ignored her and those who talked to her and ignored me. There were only a few who talked to us both and ignored the tension between us. This division split fairly logically: most of the second, third and other wives were for me and most vahosi and all those women lucky enough to be in monogamous marriages were for her. It was just the free thinkers and men who did not take sides.

Then there were those who changed sides constantly. This last group would speak to you today and if you were silly enough to open your heart to them, you would soon discover that they did not, after all, know who you were; they had never, of course, spoken to you. Then, there were the inflamers. Their work was to throw in a log here or another there to keep the fire burning. If there was the slightest risk of it dying down, they would feed it with dry grass and twigs then blow until they could blow no more, then they danced around it, ululating, and urging it on.

Amaiguru complained that because I was not letting her touch my children I must be implying that she was a witch. But how could I be independent of her, if I depended on her to look after my children? But when that rumour found it's way back to me, I again took the children to her and asked her to look after them. Not once, but three times and she refused. She always invented an excuse: she was just leaving for the river; she was going to fetch firewood; she was doing this, she was doing that. Her message was clear. But why then was she spreading rumours? However, her actions meant that now I could say without lying that it was Amaiguru who did not want to look after my children.

After this, I was even more determined not to ask her for anything. But my mortar and pestle had not yet been delivered, so I needed to borrow from someone, and because I knew that if I did not ask her first, she would accuse me of refusing to use her things, I asked her. I shall not, however, repeat her response. She was ten wasp nests all at once. Then, I went to see the headman's wife, because I did not want to divide the village any more.

I can only say that Sekuru Chitsva's first wife looked for her own troubles. She dug deep to find them, and it was not enough to keep the quarrel between us. She had to include the children. It was like watching someone committing suicide. Everybody was drawn in.

First she tried to turn Wangi and Tawa against me. They were no longer allowed to speak to me. Then they were not even allowed to respond when I said good morning. So whenever she was there, they did not answer me, but when she was not there we talked, as we had always done. How could we stop speaking just like that? We had not wronged one another. One does not wake up one morning and become an enemy. We had lived together peacefully and there was no reason why they would turn against me. If she had left the boys out of it, Sekuru might have remained unaware as he appeared not to notice our fight.

Whenever he was home, I would bring his food to her hut in the evening and then return to mine to eat. Sekuru never asked why I was not eating with them. And, I never went to complain to him that she was refusing to help me with the children, even though my third one was well on the way. I also knew that she was working on Sekuru to turn against me. Though he continued as if nothing was amiss, I think he'd long since sensed that the winds had changed direction.

If she had managed to keep the boys on her side, things might have turned otherwise, but in her zeal to turn them against me, she only managed to turn them against herself. My friends in the village advised me to do nothing, to pretend nothing was wrong and let her start the fight if she so wished. When the time came, the verdict would depend on who threw the first stone. I made sure it would not be me.

Whenever she saw the boys speaking to me, she would flay them with her tongue. Tawa, the quieter one, bore the brunt of it; but even Wangi, who had always been rebellious, could not stand up to her. The timidity that he had always shown her was transformed into a devil-may-care attitude.

At first, when there were guests, the boys ate well, and when there were no guests and Sekuru was not there, she gave them just enough to keep them alive. Then, after a while, when they were alone, she sometimes did not cook at all. She would simply disappear at meal times and the boys would go without. Perhaps it was better when she did not cook, for she only gave them a portion of sadza as big as a child's fist for the two of them, and a tiny piece of meat, which only served to sharpen their appetites and remind them of what a good cook she was. Then she would fill her own plate with sadza, meat and vegetables while the boys watched her. Their eyes would follow her hand moving between the bowl and her mouth like the eyes of hungry dogs; and afterwards, she would give her leftovers not to them but to Godo, their dog. Godo, who had once followed Tawa, now followed Amaiguru. Tawa felt betrayed.

"Eat my baby, eat," she would say to the animal. "I know you will always be loyal to me. You're not like the others, with their short memories. I'm as barren as a man and you are my only child and you will not betray me."

I kept out of her way and watched. I cooked more food, and when she was not there, the boys came, shut themselves in my hut, and ate while I sat outside and kept my eyes open. The headman's wife told me to continue cooking for the boys and to not say anything. "Food builds lasting relationships," she told me. So I cooked and gave to the boys and Amaiguru cooked and fed Godo.

Then the explosion came. It was a full moon and just after the first rains. I remember because they had just finished my sleeping hut and I had slept in it for the first time. Maybe she could not take that. Now I had two new huts while the thatch on her old cooking hut leaked.

6

Amaiguru

I had always considered all those women who sing others to be deranged animals. I pitied them as I pitied rabid dogs. Suffering, yes, but also mad and dangerous. Those they sang I looked upon as innocents, if not victims of misunderstanding or circumstances. I swore that I would never be caught singing anybody; I would rather die first. Now I know it was because, until then, I'd never had cause. Even when my first husband's mother sang me, I did not feel the need to answer back. She was mad; I was not. I looked at my sisters-in-law who sang our mother-in-law back with astonishment. I didn't understand their need to stand outside and cry their most intimate details to anyone who could hear them. How the singer and the sung could hold their heads high after such an ordeal was beyond my comprehension. But after Chinongwa came back and started going behind my back, saying things, laughing at me with strangers, people who had spat at her person when she first arrived, I started feeling as if I couldn't breathe. She went behind my back to ask her husband for a mortar and pestle that, only three seasons before, she had refused when I had offered them to her. She had also refused to let me buy her grinding stones, saying that the two that belonged to me were enough for the two of us.

I still don't know when she went to the tailor to be measured for her dresses. All I know is that one day she paraded in front of me wearing a new dress. I made no comment; I sewed my lips. Nobody had ever told me anything. If she'd come to ask me for a new dress, why would I have said no to her? All my four dresses were as good as hers. I even offered her some of my dresses to make clothes for her children. It was I who taught her how to make clothes for she didn't know how to sew when I took her in. What had I not done for her?

Both husband and wife were hatching plans behind my back. Her children, which she had always left with me whenever she went anywhere, she now left alone in the hut. What if they hurt themselves? Denying me her children was stronger than any words anyone could have thrown at me. I could feel her finger pointed at the nape of my neck.

A husband with more than one wife should not take sides— a rule that a man ignores at his peril. At first I did not say anything, waiting for a gossip to tell me what was on her mind. Nobody did, but Chinongwa was avoiding me. Yet when she returned with her brother from burying her mother, I welcomed them both with two hands. It was only after Tafadzwa had left that Baba Chitsva announced that he was going to build her a sleeping hut, and I thought it was a good thing; for once, he had taken the initiative and done something without being asked. I thought it was because there had been nowhere for her brother to sleep. When Tafadzwa was there, we had guests at the same time and two days afterwards, Baba Chitsva had left. He did not return until Tafadzwa had gone. I thought he had been absent so that we could give his hut to the in-law. The first two nights we had asked the two boys to sleep in

166

the cooking hut so that Tafadzwa could sleep in their sleeping hut. But now I know that it was Chinongwa who asked him for that extra sleeping hut.

At first, when she arrived, he had sworn never to touch her, but as she blossomed with my good food, I taught her how to seduce him, and it didn't take long before he succumbed. At first, I made her sleep with us because she was afraid of him. So, for a moon, she just slept with us—behind me, of course. He was determined not to fall for this, and I knew it and pretended that I did not know. After a moon, I put her between us from time to time.

She had learnt well. I had warned her in advance so that nothing would come as a complete surprise to her. She knew what to do. I was her tete once more. I knew when we had trapped him, but still I made him wait until it became unbearable for him. He could not hide his feelings when he found her firm, young body lodged between us. When she rubbed against him in the night, it was I who relieved him. Then after some time he no longer knew whose hands were touching him in the dark. He started looking longingly at her when he thought he was alone. I could see it in his eyes. I knew then that the meat was cooked.

The first time I was there to help her. I knew that it had to go well or everything would be lost. And it went well. I think he felt ashamed for a few days afterwards, but by then it was too late. He had drunk from the enchanted well and I knew he was going to come back for more. He was man, after all, and he had to.

Yes, he was like a rat that had escaped from the trap. The rat cannot stop thinking about the peanut butter that it has left there. It is aware that it might get caught if it goes back, but it can think of nothing else. The smell of peanut butter within its reach, intoxicates it. It circles the trap, then runs away. Far away. It congratulates itself for escaping with its life. It tells itself that it is indeed a very strong rat, and that if it had been any weaker it would never have escaped. Then, the flutter of hunger flickers again.

167

The rat draws near: looks, sees, smells, but runs away, not so far this time. And so it goes until that fatal moment when it can't help itself any longer. It closes its eyes and digs deep into the ecstasy of that peanut butter, and forgets everything—yes, just as my husband forgot his name, where he had come from, what his totem was. He forgot his morality, the resistance he had promised and made so much of in the world.

By the time the rat is sated, it is well and truly trapped. At that moment, Baba Chitsva chose to turn not against the trap but against me, blaming me, as if it was me who had set it up.

"Were we not living happily before you gave away my cattle to the first beggar who arrived? Do not bother me with women's stories and problems of your own making. You wanted a co-wife; you got one. I will not listen to burning tongues." I had nowhere to turn, no one to turn to and the bone that had planted itself in my throat was choking me.

In my first marriage, whenever I'd felt a bone in my throat, I'd always talked to my master and he'd always had the right words to remove it. When I first arrived at my second master's home and there'd been talk in the village about my sterility, the bone had reappeared; I had told my master and he too had said the right words to make it disappear. So how could I have behaved like those other women who undressed each other to the last hair in front of the whole village? I could not be like them. I knew how to make that kind of pain disappear. Talk to your master. Easy!

This time, the bone did not disappear. If anything, it grew; so that by the second day, there was no room for either food or water to pass down my throat. Even though the master went away soon after his rebuke, the sight of his young wife made me want to choke.

The night before it happened, I tossed and turned. I prayed for sleep. But when sleep came nightmares followed: my mother was there with my father. Even some whom I had never met, people

168

who had died before I was born were all there, laughing at me. Whenever I tried to reach out for my mother, she moved away. I couldn't explain anything to them. When I tried, my voice did not come out. They couldn't hear what I was trying to say. And someone was telling me to speak louder. The morning was nearly upon us, so I tried harder and harder and shouted as loudly as I could, but nothing happened. Even my boy lover was watching me. Filled with shame at the sight of me, he turned his back on me and would not look at me. But when the others left, he didn't go away, he stayed, his head bent low and I knew I had lost. When I asked him if he thought this was so, he sadly nodded his head following the others out. I had to catch him. He could explain everything for me. He was the only one who really knew me. I ran after him, but my legs were heavy, so heavy that the distance between us kept growing. I started to cry. Everyone had forsaken me, even the boy I had first loved. But, had I not betrayed him? Not once, but twice. He could never forgive me. First, he had tied my womb so that I could never give children to anyone; and now he would not help me in this, my darkest hour.

When I awoke I was wet with sweat. I was hot. My covers felt heavy and I kicked them away. No wonder I couldn't run. I drank from the gourd and then went out to pass water. The sky was so clear that the proud daughter-in-law with the faggot of wood on her head inside the moon was well-defined. On earth, there was a heavy silence; it weighed me down. I am not afraid of the night, but I could not bring myself to spit, let alone cough, for I was afraid to disturb the silence. I looked at the moon and felt the eyes of pride upon me. I wondered why the woman never took that bundle of sticks off her head. Did she not feel its weight? It looked like a heavy one too. Some people said that she'd been punished and would carry it until the end of time. I wondered what she had done to deserve such a punishment.

I went back inside, but it was a long time before sleep returned. When it did, the nightmare returned, so I knew that I wouldn't want to sleep again. The constriction in my throat would choke me.

It was after the third cock's crow when I knew that I had to do something I had sworn not to do. The moon was bright and I could see clearly, so I took out my mortar and pestle, went inside my granary and gathered as much sorghum as I could. Then I brought out a whole chirongo of water. My fear of silence had evaporated.

I poured sorghum into the mortar, then poured the water onto it, and I picked up my pestle and began pounding. At first, I could not bring myself to say anything. I had never done this before. But what if somebody heard me, came out and saw me pounding in the middle of the night? They would really think I was a muroyi. I had to sing. But how to begin? Already the sound of the pestle was ringing loud in my ears.

At first, my voice sounded as if it was coming from far away, as if in a dream, as if it did not belong to me. But after a while the words began pouring from deep within me. They chased each other out, one after the other, as if they had been imprisoned. I felt a weight falling off me, and then I was flying, flying higher and higher, reaching the heights that we only reach when a man that pleases is inside.

I told her everything that I had kept to myself. I was glad the master was not there, for though it was just between us women, when the words poured out, I was no longer in control. Husband and wife and children all received their share. Those two-faced villagers got what they deserved as well. I did not spare anyone, and by midday, when I finally finished the sorghum, I had no more voice, but the bone in my throat had disappeared. I took my sorghum to the threshing rock, spread it out to dry and went home to sleep. As soon as I laid my aching body to rest, I fell asleep and did not wake until dusk. I had just enough time to bring my sorghum in.

7

Chinongwa

W hen first I heard the pounding, it must have been well before the fourth cock's crow. I was half-asleep and everything was mixed in with my dream. It took me a while to define the noise as pounding. Even then, I dismissed it as my own imagination. Who would be pounding in the middle of the night? I was sinking back to sleep when her sharp voice pierced the still night. I jumped off the mat and sat up. At first, I thought the voice was coming from the headman's hut, but quickly I realised that it was Amaiguru. Spitting it all out. Everything.

"What was it but rags and bones when I took it in out of pity? What would it be today if I had not taken it in? Had not everyone refused it? And not without reason. Who was mad, if not me? They all said the same, but I did not listen. Her sore eyes crusty with mucus; arms and legs as thin as reeds which could break in two. A cow from dry lands where grass no longer grew. A cow that would have died at the well, had I not dragged it out so that it could breathe between gulps."

My stomach knotted. I pulled my knees in as high as I could and stared out into the moonlit darkness, holding my breath. I had heard people sing each other only three or four times in my life. It could not be happening to me. And she had placed her mortar and pestle so close to my hut that I could not miss one word.

"Thanks to me, it shed its skin like a python that had swallowed a goat. And was it not a naked cow? I gave it drink, I gave it food and I dressed it. How many said that I should not take in an errant, starving dog? That I should not feed it with milk because tomorrow it would bite the hand that fed it? Maidei, Maidei, Maidei, why did you not listen? They told you that an animal will never be thankful. They knew what they were talking about. I should have listened."

I was that cow, that errant dog, that python. She was calling herself Maidei; the maiden name she had sworn to forget.

"Now it has forgotten what I did for it, because it is empty-headed. Why is that? Because whenever it shits, it leaves some of its brains behind. If it didn't, it would not be shitting in the well from which it drinks. Now that the water in the well is no more good for drinking, the dog should not be surprised. Either it is going to stop drinking and die of thirst, or it will have a bloated stomach. The die is cast and there is no more going back."

I could not believe it was Amaiguru. She had told me she did not believe in singing—and warned me that I should never sing anybody because it was a degrading act. She had told me that if ever I felt the need to sing anyone, it was time to go and talk to that person. I had promised to, if ever I felt the need. And now what was I hearing? I stuck my earlobes into my ears like I used to do when I was small, but still her voice penetrated through to me. "I was a clean well, which overflowed with sweet, fresh water, water that every passerby appreciated and remembered seasons to follow. Now that this animal has had enough of my water and has soiled it, those who drink knowingly or unknowingly are all going to suffer.

172

I am no longer responsible. Nobody is innocent. Those that soil and those that watch without lifting a finger are also guilty. When you see a dog polluting the well that you drink from, is it not wise to say, 'Stop! I drink from there. Leave it clean, for tomorrow I shall be thirsty!' If we watch and encourage the dog to come again the next day and shit some more into the well, let us not be surprised about what happens to us."

I was sure she was referring to the headman and his wife. Though she could not say anything to them or bar them from her list, she did not like the fact that they went on talking to me, nor that the headman's wife had lent me her mortar and pestle. They were being sung because of me. Were they going to blame me for this? But why was she singing the headman's family? One should never rub them the wrong way. Did she not know she was digging her own grave?

"After all, this errant dog, I did not want it for myself, but for him. In one act, I saved it and lit a fire for him. I thought he deserved some extra warmth. Now that one has had enough food and drink and the other enough warmth, both shit on me."

I was glad Sekuru was not there to hear that. That would have driven him into murdering someone. After all, he had never asked for a maiden from anyone. Now she was blaming him. Just as well he was not there, or spears would have been thrown.

"That first child of yours. Who washed his body, and whose dress did we tear to wrap him in? And who dug the grave? Was it my flesh and blood? Now that we have enough to eat and drink, we forget where we came from. None of your own cared for you. The moment they got the food they wanted, they never came back to see you. If you had died, they would not have cared. They sold you like a cow that was for slaughter. Not even your tete came back to see you once. All those seasons that you stayed here without masungiro, you would have thought that your people would have come to see if you were alive. Nobody except me cared for you.

Even your master did not care a scrap. He found you revolting. I suffered from his hand because of you."

What a relief that the children had gone on sleeping after I assured them all was well. What a relief they were too young to understand, even if they were listening. I was cold but could not bring myself to change position. Was I afraid that she would know I had moved?

"I say to you, with all the animals and those listening as my witnesses, you will live to regret what you are doing to me. I swear on my dead mother's grave. My mother who was of the monkey totem, and I who am of the lion totem. I swear to you the strings between us are broken. If we had been of the same blood, we would have killed a cow to break the blood ties between us. I would have provided the cow willingly."

I started praying that the boys were not listening to all this. How was I going to face them tomorrow?

"To all those who have betrayed me, today I cut the strings of attachment; he whom I thought was my master, I now cut the strings of attachment; those who were animals and I turned into humans, I cut the strings of attachment. If I die with this bone in my throat, the whole family will dance to the harvest song. Nobody, I repeat, nobody will be spared."

I listened to all this and more, barely breathing. When she finally stopped pounding, the sun was overhead. Her voice was so hoarse it could hardly be heard. She must have filled five or six harvest baskets of sorghum. Her hands must have been full of blisters. I was naked. I do not think she had forgotten anything about me. My hair, my breasts, my legs, my nails and the dirt in them … everything. All she knew about me and everything that I had told her in confidence. She had told them that I walked in the dark of the night. They were all going to think that I was a muroyi who was possessed every night. They had all listened. I was even afraid to go to the well. Where was I going to look? She had undressed

174

me in front of the whole village. She had never done it before. The other women in the village who had done it to each other, she had always laughed at them and said it was just as demeaning to the singer as the sung. If she had come to me, I would have explained why I was trying to get my independence. After all, I had always confided in her.

I knew that people were going to be looking at me wherever I went, knowing that Sekuru had refused to touch me, that she had had to put me between him and her when they went to sleep, and that it was only after more than two moons that he finally took me. Oh, how naked I was! In the beginning, when Sekuru finally took me, I had told her all the details. Even though I had not wanted to because I was too ashamed when he took me, every morning she would ask me about it and I would tell her everything. Everything. Now she had told the whole village. And not only that, she had sung that Sekuru had said that lying with me was like sleeping with a lifeless fish. I was cold and dead. He would not have liked to know that what he had said had been repeated to the village. But he was not there and, most likely, would never know. But how naked I was!

The boys had heard it. The headman and his wife had heard it. I did not mind about his wife so much because she knew what had been happening, but all the other women … and the children, and all the other men in the village. Now everybody knew everything.

I did not even know that all the other men were always dying to get to their wives until after my second child, when some of the women started talking about those things to me at the well. They said their husbands did not leave them alone even when they were sick. It was a discovery to me because Sekuru was not at all like that. It was usually Amaiguru who would tell me to go and sleep in his hut before he went to sleep, or after he went to sleep—depending on his mood. She had taught me when and where to touch him. When the children were small, she would keep them and tell me to go and sleep with him so that I could have children and, therefore, the respect of all the people in the village. So when she told me to go to him I went and I aroused him like she had taught me. Up to then, I had always thought that all women went to arouse their husbands so that they could have children and the respect of the village.

I never repeated what the other women told me to Amaiguru, neither did I tell the other women what happened in our home. Even when they teased me and wanted to know whether I liked it or not. They would ask whether Amaiguru and I fought and cheated on each other, and whether Sekuru visited us in our own huts, or whether we went to him. They wanted to know how many nights a week I had with him. But I always kept my lips tight because Amaiguru had warned me that they would go and spread it through the village. Any woman who is worth herself does not divulge such things. So when the other women scratched at me, I would laugh with them, but I never told them what the arrangement was. But the terrible thing I had done was to indirectly make them believe that Sekuru's hunger for me was endless.

I spent the day in my hut. How could I let myself be seen? I knew that by that afternoon they would all be talking about me. How well she had planned. She could not have done it better. The only thing that I did was to sneak to the well to get some water for my children and for cooking.

I did not know what to do. I could sing back, but my mortar and pestle were not yet delivered. The man was going to deliver them this week. Was he going to come that day? If he came, I was not going to see him. He could leave everything outside and I would get them in at dusk. But if he had heard, then he would not be coming that day.

The strange thing was that I did not cry. Ever since I had come, every time Amaiguru had done or said anything that had pained me, I had cried. When the other women in the village teased me more than usual, I cried. I was known for crying, and was teased even more for that. And now, after her singing, all I wanted to do was cry, but my eyes were dry with shock. I sat down on the mat in my sleeping hut and waited and waited for the tears to come, but nothing happened; when I went into the cooking hut, I used some wet twigs to provoke them, but again nothing happened.

After eating, Tinashe went outside to play and, from the voices, I could tell that he was playing with the headman's children. After a while there was nobody and I knew that they had gone to the headman's house. I could hear footsteps crossing my yard from time to time, but I did not look to see who it was. Nobody called greetings either. I waited until dusk to go to the well.

***

Some had advised me to ignore her and others thought I should not let her walk over me; if I did not sing her back then she was always going to treat me like a child and not like a co-wife. I did not know what to do. I had nobody close to talk to. If I had not promised never to return to my home, maybe I would have gone then. Nobody would have followed me, for not even Sekuru cared. How I wished Mother was still alive. I needed her now more than ever.

When I thought of her and recalled that she had loved me, I finally cried. I also felt angry with her for betraying me by dying— just when I had discovered how much she loved me. She would have known what to do about Amaiguru. I tried to imagine what her advice would have been. I felt like an orphan, lonely and alone.

I knew it was no use going to my father to say, "My vahosi has just sung me. Do I sing back or not?" Would he even hear me? If he did, would he answer? Yet I was not angry with him. Once I had hated him, but now I knew that what he had done was normal. He was a man and he had acted like a man. Men say strong words. They take action, make tough decisions. All this with a force that should not send any doubts whatsoever. They are not to waver or stutter. Whether or not they like the decisions they are taking, they are required always to look bold and decided.

When real men don't agree on a hot point, they solve it physically, not verbally. Instead of singing each other, they have it out. If they are inside when a disagreement starts, they go outside and finish it off with their bodies and fists. The one with the real balls and a long member will win. But the father that I last saw was not a real man. Were he a real father, he might have come and told my husband and Amaiguru that I was not to be treated in this way.

So for a week after Amaiguru sung me, I was ashamed to go out and avoided her. But my mind was always busy. Whether to sing back or not. If it had been someone else, I might have gone to Amaiguru to ask her what I was to do: she had always given me advice. But now she was the problem. While I pondered the question, I prepared my sorghum, just in case.

Many advised me not to tell Sekuru and pretend in front of him that nothing had happened. I had already resolved to do this. Whenever I was forced to meet her, I greeted her as usual and she gave me a look that made me freeze. Lately, she had become still harsher with all of us, even Sekuru. I was afraid to give the boys food in case she caught me red-handed, so I would give it to them in the afternoons when she did not cook. She knew that I was feeding them. When she asked if they were eating in my house, I denied it, but I knew she was waiting to catch me. I had to be careful. After that, there were days she spent in front of her hut, not going anywhere but not cooking either, watching to see if I would give them food. On such days, the boys had nothing to eat. It was not my fault. I could not do anything about it. Luckily, the first berries after the first rains were appearing, so during the day they ate as much as they could and drank a lot of water. It keeps hunger away. And they started accepting food in the village while I looked the other way.

On the evenings Sekuru was there, they were given food. I would take my sadza for him to her hut. Once when I took it in the afternoon when he was not there, she threw it away in front of Godo. So when I knew that Sekuru was out, I no longer took him his sadza. Then she asked me why I had not brought him food; I had to cook for him, she said, even when I knew he wouldn't be there. Often, when Sekuru was not home, she would eat the food that I had cooked and feed the left-overs to Godo, so the boys would go without. When things were really bad, the boys escaped to school every day. Sekuru did not stop them, but spent the morning minding his cattle.

It was just after the second rains, when we had sowed, that I was forced to act. Because this was the period when we were waiting for the first weeds, and there was nothing much to do. The women would bring in the last firewood and the men would repair the huts. At that time, Sekuru went to Bikita, and as soon as he'd left, it became hotter—blazingly so. Amaiguru became possessed. Nobody, not one moving thing, was spared: the boys, my children, my hens, me. Even Godo got kicked whenever he was in the way.

The village started its slow humming, almost silently at first. She was not the same person any more. Every morning she swept her whole yard and woe betide anyone who dared drop a fruit skin, a leaf, even a footprint on it! Those who trespassed were skinned alive with the whip of her tongue. Not even Tinashe and baby Tendai were allowed into her yard. She told them that if they strayed into it, she would poison them because she was a witch. Even though Tinashe did not understand what she meant—having seen only three seasons—he understood enough to know that he had to avoid that yard. He only had to see her coming to know that he must run—dragging his little brother behind him. Whenever she saw him, she would shout encouragement:

"Faster, faster, to its mother! Or I shall turn it into a dry cadaver while it walks! Faster, faster, child of a dog, or you will not see another summer! Faster, faster, away from the witch! Your mother warned you: I am the muroyi, the destroyer of true love between husband and wife, the eater of live children! Be gone, to its wretched mother, to where it belongs!"

When she swept her yard, I think she wanted to draw me into a fight. She swept all her dirt into my yard and left it there. As if that was not enough, she took most of the yard and left me with very little. Before, I used to sweep nearly up to her hut. Indeed, she had told me that I could have most of her yard because she didn't need all that space any more. I think it was a trick to make me do most of the sweeping. Now, with her newfound energy, she swept away my yard. The children who used to play under the mango tree could no longer do so because it now belonged to her. Since she had planted that tree, what could I do? It was up to me to make Tinashe and baby Tendai understand.

And my hens were dirtying her yard:

"If your hens leave droppings, you should sweep them away before they blind my eyes!"

How could I spend the whole day chasing my hens from her yard? Any mess was blamed on my hens. Whenever she saw turds she would call me to sweep them away. Whenever she found my hens in her yard, she sent them flying back home with a kick. Once I even put them inside my hut to avoid any problems, but by the end of the day the hut smelt so badly that we had to go outside. Instead of giving me relief, I had to remove all the droppings and then re-polish the floor with cow dung, which I had done only two days before. In the end, I decided to give the chicks away to whoever wanted them and to eat the rest of the hens one by one. This way I could at least enjoy them.

I spent as much time as I could away from home. I made sure I took my children with me. But whenever I came back, she was there, sitting in front of her hut, watching my comings and goings like an old vulture waiting for a weak animal to fall. I couldn't take it any more.

Those days were the longest of my life. I was not living but surviving. Night never came. I wished I didn't have to go back home during the day but I had to cook and let baby Tendai take his nap. All the while, the question of whether to sing her or not would not leave me in peace. At night I tossed and turned, and when morning broke, I did not feel the relief that sleep is supposed to bring. Just hearing the noise from the first birds telling me it was time to face the day was enough to make my stomach knot. Also, I knew I would not be capable of pounding much sorghum. I was now heavy with child. So for a week I did nothing.

In the end, it was her actions that changed the situation. By then, I had already eaten three of my hens. I still had ten more to go, seven of them with small chicks. Since that time I forced myself to eat my hens, I've never enjoyed chicken again.

It was after she had called me three times to sweep away hen droppings one morning that I prepared my sorghum for the next morning. Just five or six mortars were going to give me enough time to empty my chest.

I did not sleep for fear of not waking in time to sing her. When I heard the first cock's crow, I got dressed but thought it too early to start. I sat on my mat and listened to my heart pounding as if it wanted to destroy me. Mixed with the night noises and the wind's howling, I wished I didn't have to go out there, but by the second cock's crow I was out, dragging my mortar from under the hozi. I was relieved to find it, for while I had lain awake I thought I'd heard Amaiguru dragging it away.

The night was chilly, the moon still and clear. The huts watched me silently like malevolent sentinels. The mango trees shook their branches at me with disapproval while the wind hissed threats. Though I tiptoed, I had the impression I was making enough noise to wake the whole village. My heart did not stop pounding.

181

I hurried, fearing Amaiguru could hear all this; if she came out and told me to put the mortar back in its place, I was sure to obey her and run back to my hut.

I had worried about what I was going to say and where I was going to start, but when finally I began pounding, the words fought each other in their haste to come out of me. At first tears ran down my cheeks, but as I continued they ceased and my voice pierced the night. All stood still while I pounded and pounded. When I realised I did not have enough sorghum, I decided to keep pounding until everything became powder. I did not feel tired; my hands moved independently of me and my voice punctuated the pounding.

I told her everything:

"Your old dresses that you used to make me wear, dresses that earned me the nickname ishwa, 'flying termite' because they were too long for me, you made me wear them, knowing how ridiculous I looked. Or maybe you laughed with everybody else. You had four dresses while I had only one. When I told you I had to sit and wait for it to dry, do you remember your reply? 'Wash your dress first before you wash your other things, so that by the time you finish, your dress will be dry.' You did not say, 'We shall buy you another one.' I had hoped so much for you to say that. I was the only person who was washing her clothes with almost nothing on.

"I know what you said about me in the village. As stupid as the village idiot. You told them my brains were like a sieve and had to be refilled daily, that I was not able to look after my children on my own. I have decided not to give you my children any more because I do not want you to claim that you raised them. I am their only mother. When I made the decision to raise them by myself, you told me that I had accused you of witchcraft. Now you know why.

"I'm ashamed of how you are ill-treating the boys and making them starve in their own home. Whatever you think, the whole village knows it and is humming with disapproval. They see it. Sekuru is going to know that you are not feeding them. He's not blind. Is that a big heart? Giving all the food to the dog and letting the children starve? I'm going to start giving them food myself if you do not cook for them. I'm not going to watch them starve in their own home. If you'd told me that you were tired of cooking for them, I would have offered to do it. Instead, you watch me every day to make sure I'm not giving them food. Now listen to me, from now on, I'm going to give them as much food as they want and I dare you stop me."

The longer I sang, the more courageous I became. I felt my fear of her dropping off me like a heavy crust of clay and I felt free and light. Because the burden that had been weighing me down had shaken off, I felt myself soaring to unheard of heights.

"The Chinongwa that you used to treat like your slave is no more. She is gone, buried and will never come back. You're just a vahosi and I do not have to obey you. From today, I'm going to stop killing my hens and they are going to walk freely because you do not own this earth. I'm not going to spend the whole day sweeping droppings from your yard. This is a Chitsva yard. When you came here, you did not bring it on your head. You are a stranger here. Just like me. But my children are of the Shava totem and the name Chitsva. I do not want to see anybody chasing my sons from their yard again. If one day Baba Chitsva gets tired of us, he will send you and me back where we came from, but these children will remain here."

Nothing was going to stop me now. First my head, then my shoulders, my torso, my whole body soared, and the clay coat fell down. I felt dizzy from the height and decided I wasn't going to come down again. I didn't want that heavy coat again. Ever. When I looked down, all was small while I continued to grow.

"I am tired of being told how you looked after me and how you fed me. I did not ask you to take me to give to your husband. If you had left me alone I would have gone back to my people and found someone who appreciated me instead of an old man who does not know what is good for him. If it were not for me he would have nothing but two children. What do I know as to why he does not love me like other men love their wives? Maybe you should tell me why. Maybe someone gave him a love potion so that he has eyes but for her. Otherwise how could he close his eyes to your ill-treating him and his children? The chief respects him more than you do."

"You're fooling yourself about breaking the string that attached us. I was never attached to you. You tell everybody everything about me. Do you think I have nothing to say about you? If I want, there are many things that I could say. Things that you told me about the people in the village. Things about your ex-husband and your family. You are not as good-hearted as you pretend to be. You want to blame me for everything that went wrong in your life."

It was just as well I was out there alone. The anger that rose as those words came out was choking. If she were anywhere nearby, I would have pounded her instead. So I pounded harder into the mortar.

"You gave me to your husband because you wanted to thank him, but what good was that to me? Why did you not give him one of your own people? And if you were so good-hearted, why did your own people refuse you a maiden for your first husband? Whenever I am out with him, people think he is my grandfather, and he pretends that he is my grandfather. You do not feel ashamed when you go anywhere with him. He had not seen four tens and eight seasons when you married him. Yet you do not stop saying how good and kind you are. And he does not even love me. Instead, he loves and respects you, who is barren. You promised me that once I had given him children, he was going to love and respect me. Is he loving me now? Have I not given him two children already, not counting the one who left us? You lied to me. You do not want him to love me, do you?"

"You're jealous of me because I have children and you do not. You used to tell me you were going to make me beautiful so that he would have eyes only for me, but he only looks at you. You made me wear your ugly dresses so that I can never be beautiful. You keep his money. You have a bigger plot than mine so that after harvest you can go to the store and exchange your grain for more things than I can.

"Listen to me well, and do not forget what I'm going to tell you. If you see me dying, do not help me. Take your help, your good heart and your good mind and use it for yourself. You're in desperate need of help.

"I am tired of everything: living with you, being married to an old man, not being loved, and you telling me off every day as if I am your child. I am tired of sweeping droppings from your hens and you watching me every day. I want you to leave me alone. I wish I had never met you."

Because the price I paid for singing back was high, even today, I still wonder if I should not have swallowed my pride and kept quiet.

Two days later, I lost the baby girl that I had been carrying. When the baby arrived, the midwife woke Amaiguru, who said she was coming, but she never did. It was a long struggle and everybody thought I would die with the baby inside me. I only remember the headman's wife telling me that I must not leave the small ones alone. The baby was still alive when she came into the world, but she did not survive long, not even to utter a cry. When the headman's wife went to tell Amaiguru what had happened, her door was tied up and we did not know where she'd gone. It was the headman's wife, the midwife and some elderly women who went to the wetlands to bury my first daughter that I was neither to see nor hold.

For a week I was not able to go out and see where they had buried her.

Amaiguru, when she came back, did not offer me condolences. She behaved as if nothing was amiss. She was that bold. I was ready to accept false condolences. Up to now, when I feel guilt about what became of her, I think of the daughter that I lost and the guilt disappears. Nothing would be the same between us again.

8

Amaiguru

When the child sang me, I felt my strength ebb out of me. When people I'd expected to console me did not come to see me, I knew it was time to go. It was the end.

By the time the master got home a week after the singing, he already knew what had happened during his absence. Once more I waited for him to balm my wounded soul and patch up my pride, but he acted as if all was well. He could tell that my heart was bleeding but he preferred to remain blind. I waited a long time, a whole moon. Either he was with me or he was not. And if he was not, there was no need for me to pretend.

I went to the headman to lodge a complaint. I did not want to live with one who wished I were not there, but I wanted him to pay me back for the service that I had rendered. I had looked after his children as if they were from my own womb. I wanted the headman to give me my own plot of land far from him and his ladylove.

When the dare was convened, he took offence. All I had ever done for him was forgotten. I was his enemy. They had to tie him up for he wanted to kill me with a spear. I was an ox that had outlived its use but still needed to be fed, so he wanted to get rid of me.

Early the next morning, the villagers came to my hut to watch him put the dombo I was to take to my people in my tswanda. Though some pretended to cry, they were satisfied. I did not protest but took the basket calmly and sat it in front of me. "I am not going to ask for the cattle I sent to your people," he declared. "I am not chasing you away. You have chased yourself away from my home. I never came to get you from your people; you will therefore go back the way you came."

Though I did not want to see my people, I wished Baba Chitsva had gone to get his cattle back. I was going to walk the jungle while my family grew fat on the cattle from me. The villagers praised his generosity. Women ululated. Once more I felt slighted. He was the generous one. I, who had looked after his children and found him a wife, was to be sent to slaughter.

I then told them, "I shall not bother you any longer than is necessary my elder ones. I feel I have done what I was brought here for. The children do not need me any longer and the master has someone to cook for him. I shall neither linger nor look for battle. My heart is clean. Let those who deserve it carry their heavy load. When the time comes, Musiki will know how to avenge me."

When they had all filed out, disappointed with my tearless eyes, I went to my sleeping hut and lay down my bones to rest and think.

When I left my first husband, I had somewhere to go. Even though I could not go from one husband to the other but went to my people first, I had a final destination, Chitsva. I did not tell my people right away and I remember laughing at them. They had two fears, looking after me and returning my husband's cattle, as my womb had refused to open. They were angry with me as well. How dare I not open my womb! I had come back to create problems

188

for them. They wanted those cattle for marrying off their sons. My allotted brother treated me like a porcupine that has forced its way into a rabbit hole.

It was only when they discovered that my husband did not want his danga back that I felt the atmosphere relax. When I left to go and marry Chitsva, there were smiles and laughter all around. I had once more become a good girl; I was forgiven the sin of being barren. "It is the axe that chops that forgets, not the tree."

Like a witch, Chitsva was now sending me away in the middle of the green season. Like the barren woman I was … no child was going to cry for me. No child was going to hold onto my dresses and try to stop me from leaving. Even the dog didn't care for me. It was to remain with them. If I walked into the first river and drowned, nobody would miss me or cry for me.

I had always thought that if ever it came to this, I would put an end to my life. I was not going to do it in his home, for it would be demeaning to my person. No matter how unbearable things get, I have always known how to hold my head high. When my brothers refused me a maiden for my first husband, I never went back to ask them for one for my second. When my first husband's people took a second wife for him to shame me, I did not stay to see myself being laughed at—I left. Even after he followed to try and persuade me to come back, I refused. I knew that once his new wife had given him children, there would be nothing to hold him to me. He was going to slide nearer to her than me; I didn't need any more humiliation. The only respectable solution for both of us was for me to leave.

Alas, this time there was no Chitsva waiting for me to look after his children. I had sworn to my family that I didn't want to see them at my funeral. I had cut the string that attached me to them. I was not going to them now to demean myself, saying that I had finally changed my mind and they could now bury me. It was too late for that and I had no regrets. There was no need for them to shed false tears for me when they had never cared. They did not care for me, and they knew that I knew it.

I had never imagined that Chitsva would throw me out like milk that had turned in the sun. When I took Chinongwa in and there were those who warned me that I'd just dug my own grave, I didn't believe them. How could I, when he'd always shown me respect? I, a barren woman, who'd bled for nothing … for like a normal woman, I bleed.

Was this not once more my boy lover's work? Had he not taken me away from my first husband? And what did I do when he took me away? I went straight to another man, despite my promise to him. Yet I kept asking him to open my womb. Why was he to open my womb for another man? So that I could give to another that which I never gave him? Now he had chased me away again. I was trying to blame others for what was happening. It was not the fault of the child. It was I who took her in for Chitsva so that my boy lover would forgive me. I had hoped that after all these seasons and the punishments he had inflicted on me, it was enough.

Though I had no clear idea where I was going, I knew I had to go far away from the village. There was not much to be done. I just had to leave a few things to a few trusted people who were scattered here and there, pay the few debts that I had and then walk away.

When I left, I felt the triumph of those who had told me that I was digging my own grave. I could feel their glee. They were going to celebrate the fruit of their prophecy. I did not begrudge them their euphoria, for that was what it became. They had, for all these last six seasons since Chinongwa came, waited for this to happen. Six seasons is a long time to wait, so they deserved their glory. If they could, they would have killed a fat cow to celebrate. Some, in my presence, pretended otherwise, but there were many who did not hide their feelings. I had offended all womankind in the village and its surroundings. I now took the flogging I deserved.

190

The vahosi believed I had offended by my generosity. Their husbands did not stop reminding them. Some owed their co-wives to my taking Chinongwa for Baba Chitsva. Whether their husbands would have had a second wife anyway could never be known.

Yes, there was the possibility that my taking Chinongwa might have encouraged a few men to go off in search of second wives, but Chinongwa was not the first second wife. At the same time, one understands the need for a scapegoat. If I was the reason why those men took second wives, then it could not be the fault of the first wives. It could not be said that the first wife was not efficient under the covers, or bored her husband, or was sickly or aging quickly.

Chinongwa was now the root of every woman's problems. Yet the more wives a man had, the larger his standing was supposed to be. One just had to look at all those wives. If the wives were always pregnant or suckling little ones, that man was the bull of all bulls. All the other men could not measure themselves against him. Men who said he was mad were dismissed as jealous or without prowess.

Chitsva had thrown me to the dogs and they were charging for the attack. Not just biting, but tearing me apart. I could understand their need to rent and tear. One day is long enough to wait. One afternoon is an eternity. But what did it matter? The enemy was there in front of them. Each of them could do exactly what they wanted. Those who wanted me raw could have me without worrying or getting in the way of those who were cooking me first. All appetites and tastes were satisfied. Is there a better feast than the downfall of the one who set herself above you?

I deserved to be chased away during the dark of the green season. I was leaving my crops flowering like wild seed in the field. My departure would calm the village. The vahosi would feel avenged at last. My master would be relieved to see my back. Chinongwa could now have her independence, husband and children to herself. Wangi and Tawa, now that they could wash themselves, did not need me any more. Even my dog, the one that I thought knew to whom he belonged, no longer needed me. Tawa would look after him. There was nothing behind; I could only look forward.

The village was now scattered with jackals that had smelt the blood of weakening prey. If they got me, they would surely not let go. Strength is in numbers. Many would not dare look me in the eyes, but now that they had tasted blood, and they were a pack, they were not going to rest until they had my head as well. I could only push forward until I was far away and safe.

I have said I shall return for those of my things that I've left behind, but I know very well that I'm not coming back. I know some will start using my things right away. Some will not touch them for a respectable period, then they will excuse themselves, saying that it's better to use them rather than let them rot. They will be right. I am not coming back.

The child will use my zvirongo for brewing beer or fetching water as she pleases. I hope she will understand that I left all that for her. I have nothing against her. Poor child. She does not know her left hand from her right, and now she is alone. Maybe Baba Chitsva, now that I am not there, will give her the respect that she craves. Now that I have gone, she will realise I had nothing against her.

I shall try to go away with a clean heart so that, wherever I go, they will receive me with hearts just as clean. I know why I shall never find peace. It's my own doing. If I hadn't made that promise to my boy lover, I would, by now, have had children and found peace.

"I give myself to you, my love. Help me to not have any other man touch me. If you want me with you, take me now; I am ready to come. I am tired of this life. My heart is pure for I have forgiven all. I am tired and need to rest."

9

Chinongwa

When Sekuru came back after I had sung her, there was a period of grace when things appeared calm. At least from the outside. I started wondering if we were not coming back to the peaceful times of yore. I bathed myself in this tranquility. If things were going to be peaceful, then I was going to have my old life back, plus my independence. I would not look after the guests and I would not be obliged to look after the boys. For I knew well that without Amaiguru I would have to look after Sekuru, Wangi and Tawa, the usual guests, and my children. I had never cared for the cattle either, and as Amaiguru folded increasingly into herself, I was discovering all her duties. So, if tranquility returned, and there was peace between us, I could have both my independence and peace of mind.

Amaiguru kept cooking for Sekuru, but only when he was there. Whenever he was away, she didn't cook and the boys came to eat with me. They were not hiding from her any more. The trouble was that I did not always know when Sekuru had gone out. At times I sent his food to her house and began eating with my children, only to see Wangi and Tawa staring at me from the outside. Only then would I discover that Sekuru was away for the day or the afternoon. Amaiguru would sit calmly inside her hut, eating the food that I had brought for Sekuru. When I talked to the headman's wife, she told me to cook for the boys every day.

Maybe it was because of food that, little by little, the boys moved out of her hut and into mine. I took to leaving food for them even if they were not around. I would put it in an earthenware bowl next to the hearthstone to keep warm. Whenever they came, they untied the door and ate.

Amaiguru continued to cook for Sekuru but she was not talking to me. Only in front of the guests did we pretend all was well. As the weeding had started, we did not see each other much. She would be gone to her plot before sunrise while I was feeding the little ones. When Sekuru was absent, she didn't come back for lunch because she prepared beans or rice for herself for the day. The boys would go with the cows or to school, but I had to come back to cook for my children. So, when she demanded a dare with the headman, we were all surprised. Maybe not Sekuru. I didn't go because she had named Sekuru, not me, as the accused. They advised me not to go because it would look as if Sekuru and I were both against her. Most of what was said I heard afterwards.

She demanded that Sekuru compensate her for having looked after his children as if they were hers. She swore that if nothing was done, once dead, she was going to come back and haunt him and his children. Even now, one wonders if that is not why Wangi has never got married and is still wandering in the woods as if he has no home. Nobody knows exactly where he is, or whether or not he is still alive. Amaiguru also demanded that she got her name cleared because I, his other wife, had accused her of witchcraft.

Apparently, Sekuru exploded and told all assembled that he had never loved her. I felt embarrassed for her when I heard that. I knew

194

he had never loved me, but to think that he had never loved her either was beyond me. She was a beautiful woman. I had been told that the mother of Wangi and Tawa was even more beautiful, and men had refused to marry her because of her beauty, but then I'd never seen her. A woman more beautiful than Amaiguru? Sekuru should not have said anything like that. And in front of the dare too. I'd never had any pride, but Amaiguru needed it to survive.

"I took you out of pity, woman. Why do I have to pay a second danga for you? The danga that I sent to your family, was it for your dried womb? Did I not know that you had knots inside it? That danga was because you were going to look after my children. Now you bring me a dare. I paid five head of cattle for sterile and used goods and today I am the accused! Were you a virgin to deserve five head? Do listen to this, my ancestors. Have we ever seen doings like this? Is this not a sign of the world standing on its head?"

They said Sekuru bellowed like an angry bull. He tried to assault Amaiguru in front of everyone. The men were obliged to pin him down and tie him up until the dare was finished. Amaiguru kept her calm throughout.

"Go where you came from and see if I follow you. You came here alone and you will go back alone. You know the way. You, the headman, come at sunrise and witness me putting dombo in her tswanda. All you assembled, you are also invited to witness."

If I could, I would have made Sekuru change his mind. If he did that, Amaiguru was sure to go. She would never argue or refuse the stone like some other women. And her crops, what was going to happen to them? Even after the dare, she went to weed in her plot. I wouldn't have gone on weeding if I knew my husband was sending me away.

The next morning, when I heard people arriving, I went to her hut. It was just a witnessing and anyone could go. I hoped someone would stop him, but to those who tried to convince him to wait

195

until she had harvested what she had sowed, he promised them blood and more.

It was wrong. You do not send away your wife in the middle of the rainy season. I knew that it was not my doing and I would never have sent anybody away in such conditions, but I still feel guilty. If I had not been there to cook and look after the boys, maybe Sekuru would have waited until after the rainy season—or never driven her away. After all, he had brought her to look after his children, and she had done so; and, though they were older now, they were boys and still needed someone to look after them.

I wished I didn't know that she had nowhere to go. She had cut herself off from her people and had sworn that she was never going back to them. She had said she did not want to be mourned or buried by them. How could she now just go back? Seeing the green fields before her, she had scorched the ground she'd come from. Now that she had been barred from those green fields, there was nothing but desert for her to return to. She had forgotten that a woman owns no cave. She is a stranger in her own home and a stranger in her husband's home. She lives in these homes by invitation only.

As I watched her over the last few days, when she was tying all her things together and preparing to leave, my heart went out to her. If I had not been afraid of her I would have said something, offered a few comforting words. But I was afraid and I spent as much time as I could in the fields and came back as late as I could, just after dark so that I didn't have to see her.

Even Wangi and Tawa were sorry to see her in that state. They had suffered at her hands, but I don't think they had forgotten all those seasons when she had been like a mother to them: when she had cooked for them, put balms on their sores and spent sleepless nights with them. Ever since her arrival, she had spent more time with them than their father had done. He was away most of the time, looking after his patients or visiting his relatives. Even when

196

he was there, he had hardly spent much time at home. Occasionally, he had taken the boys out for the night to hunt and he had taught them how to set traps for the animals; occasionally, he had also gone fishing with them, but most of the time they had been with Amaiguru. When they brought animals which they had caught in their traps, it was to her that they gave them; it was she who sang and danced to the hunting song in praise of the hunters. She knew when they were sick or depressed and she knew when they were tired or had been fighting. She knew when to keep quiet and when to talk to them. With Wangi, she had known when to keep her distance and when to laugh with him. She knew his moods better than anybody else. She had known how to handle him just as much as she had known how to handle Sekuru.

***

Now, all was finished and wasted, and the boys knew they were losing the only mother they ever had. But, like me, they could not express their feelings because the last moons had been too troubled. A barrier had come up and enclosed each of us. We just had little peep holes to see what the other was doing. We could see their sorrow or count their misfortunes, but we couldn't talk to or touch them. So the boys dragged their feet while wearing their sorrowful masks and I tried to avoid everybody, carrying my guilt with me wherever I was. I couldn't look her in the face. While a few weeks ago I had not been able to look at her out of fear, now I avoided her out of guilt and pity.

I could not stand the villagers, who were congratulating me on my imminent freedom. Most of the second, third or fourth wives couldn't help but follow me to ask when she was actually leaving. They wanted to share my joy with me. My triumph was theirs. But I was not feeling joyful; I didn't find anything to rejoice in. Instead, I only felt more confused. If I had not wanted to take

197

my independence, I told myself, which was the reason the war had started, she would not be leaving. I also wondered whether or not I should ask Sekuru to let her stay. But, of course, I didn't dare to do so in case he did the same to me. People were forever making decisions that affected my life and I was forever feeling guilty. There were times I wanted to climb the hilltop and scream my innocence to the whole world.

It took Amaiguru more than a week to do her packing. She left some of her things with neighbours. They later told me she was going to stay with one of her sisters until she found somewhere else to go.

From somebody so full of care, who had taken me for her 'wonderful' husband, she had turned into a bitter, scorned woman, and then into a wet hen, all in less than one season. Seeing her tying her things up and giving them away, watching her walk silently around, her shoulders falling, was painful. I wondered if in the end I didn't prefer the vicious, wronged woman. Hating her had been preferable to feeling for her and not being able to do anything. Even my children, who a few weeks ago had been running away from her, stared at her as if she was a maimed animal.

We ate our food and washed our dishes in silence. Even Godo sensed that something was wrong. He stopped barking. He followed his mistress around as if a voice in the air was always shouting at him. In the evening, after eating, we separated as quickly as possible and as noiselessly as we could.

Sekuru, who was the root of all this change, decided to go for a visit the morning after the dare. Once he had put dombo into her tswanda, signalling the termination of their marriage, he tied his clothes bundle, secured it on the head of his axe, swung it over his shoulder and disappeared into the bush. I didn't know where he was going or when he would return. I had never known where he went anyway. Whenever I had wanted to know, it was Amaiguru whom I asked, but those times were over now.

One morning she was gone. Though I had watched her packing and knew she was going to leave, I had expected some kind of warning or goodbye. Not this. When I came back to prepare lunch, I saw her door ajar and understood what had happened.

Suddenly, I was back home six seasons ago. Heat invaded my innards from nowhere; there was the same stomach churning and urgent need to urinate. I was back to that morning when I discovered they were going to give me away after all. I could hardly breathe and had to run outside. I was that small girl once more and I could see my mother crying quietly after we had upset the water. Me trying to get outside as quickly as I could and her fearing I was running away in the darkness. I could even smell the mixture of water and ashes. A smell from that long ago, a smell that had meant a new beginning. It was the same moment now as it had been then: the familiar was lost; it was a new world; I was alone again.

I felt the same physical fear that I had felt then. Someone who had supported me had been removed from my life. I was now to face Sekuru, Wangi, Tawa and my children by myself—and the cattle, the hens, the other villagers, the guests. How would I face all this? I wasn't ready. I did not know how to talk to Sekuru. I had never even had a conversation with him. Yes, sometimes we had laughed together about one joke or another, but Amaiguru had always been there. What was I going to do?

It was strange to think that during the last few moons, when we were not speaking any more, her presence must still have subconsciously reassured me. It was not conceivable that she had left. She was as much a fixture of the village as the rocks and hills that surrounded us. She had been immovable. But now her door was open and I could hear the hens clucking from inside her hut.

Yes, I could now speak as loudly as I wanted, and if I felt like laughing, I could laugh without fear of disturbing her. Alas, I didn't feel like laughing or speaking out loud. Instead, I felt something in my throat and I could not have spoken even if I had wanted to.

I wished the boys were not coming to eat at lunch. I wished I had nobody to cook for. I wished I had somebody to talk to. I wished the times had not changed and Amaiguru was as nice as she used to be. Maybe I didn't mind having one dress after all. If I could bring her back, I'd tell her that I didn't mind waiting for my dress to dry while I sat naked at the river. I could even wash her dresses for her if only I could have her back. Amaiguru the foster mother, the laughing one, the one who looked after my children and defended me from the villagers.

My guilt multiplied when I discovered, in going to fetch some firewood under the hozi, that she had left me nearly half of all her zvirongo. She had put them nicely under my hozi, including the one that I had always admired. The one she'd promised to give me before she died, for, since I was not her blood, her people would never give it to me, she had said. We had laughed and agreed that it was most likely to break before she died.

The tears that had refused to come earlier now flowed like a river after a storm and wouldn't stop.

When the boys came for lunch and saw her door open and the hens playing inside, they too had tears flowing like summer rivers and we did not speak to each other. We pretended to eat but did not feel hungry.

10

Baba Chitsva

It is no good living in the past. I must not blame myself for marrying the child. I did not wish it. I shall only accept responsibility for marrying my first wife Chenai. Yes, then, I was fully aware of what was happening. Yes, if after her death, they had not forced my hand, I might have had peace in my life. But who knows, I might have spent the rest of my life mourning my unborn children. I wouldn't have liked them to put a mouse on my back. Once, long back, I saw someone buried this way and I still shudder at the memory. I'm indeed thankful that I am not childless.

Even though I did not have long with Chenai, she was good enough to leave me the two boys. And, even now, I don't regret the child's children. Children make a man, but maybe Maidei was right, I did not have to do it, should not have done it, with a girl, a child who, to my mind, is never going to become a woman, whatever one does. She was a child when she came and because of my age, she will always be a child to me.

Yes, I'm not ashamed to say it: I still regret that I did not refuse her. What got into me to accept her? And now, I can no longer pretend that she is not my wife, not after Maidei left. If they respected me before they got here, I dread what they will think of me when they realise that I have a child-wife. I cannot always explain how it happened. And Maidei knew how to look after guests, how to prepare the medicines. This one, she pounds the roots without washing them properly and so there are grains of sand in the potion. Still, what can a man in my situation do except wait for death to come and, with it, the only relief?

I do not regret Maidei but one cannot comfort a childless woman unless one gives her a child. She knew before coming here that she could never be with child, that she had knots in her womb, yet she never stopped hoping.

There is a heavy, dark presence somewhere in her past. Though I never asked, I always thought she knew what it was. She did not want anyone to look too far back or too deeply. When I asked if she wanted me to search for why she was barren, she forbade me. I must admit that I was also not so keen to do so. One might find something too big to keep to one's self without losing one's head. What you do not know does not follow you home.

Since she did not want me to find out, there was no reason to stir calm waters. So maybe it is just as well she left. Who knows where it was going to lead us all? I know for sure she didn't have ngozi, for I checked that out before I married her. Even if I'd got it wrong, she could not have stayed with me for ten and six seasons without the ngozi raising its head. It was something personal and deeper, a secret she wanted to keep.

Maybe her family had given her to a dead person for appeasement. But that person would never have allowed another man to touch her. If they had given her to another man, how could they receive her danga as if she did not belong already? It was something else; I shall never know, and I prefer it that way. Now she's gone, we might as well forget the whole thing. Maybe Chenai decided to make her leave now that her children are big.

And all that fighting. I couldn't stay in my home any longer. Though both of them tried to pretend in front of me that all was well, who could be fooled? The air smelt foul, poisoned.

They told me I should give them rules, but if people do not like each other, how can anyone compel them to do so? These are sentiments that cannot be forced.

I could not choose. The child could not be sent back. When I met her mother at masungiro, I gave her my word that I was going to look after her daughter. She told me that now she'd seen me, she had peace in her mind. She told me with her own mouth that she could tell that her daughter had not married a brute as her other daughter had done. She just looked at me and knew what kind of man I was. I promised that I would never chase her daughter away. After that, my hands were tied. Since then, neither the child nor Maidei knows that I gave my word to her mother.

Would things have been different if I had told Maidei? I did not promise not to tell anyone. Though neither her mother nor I said anything about it, we both understood that I was not to tell the child about the promise. Even today, whenever I get angry with her, I sense her mother behind me reminding me of my promise. Maybe if Maidei had known that I could not send the child away, she would have known to avoid fighting with her; she was not a stupid woman. She lost a battle without knowing what she was up against. Had there been a fair choice between the two, Maidei was a wife, and the child, well, she remains a child.

And yet, while Maidei was the wife, the child was a mother. Could I have chased her away if I hadn't given my word? And the children? Tinashe had seen only three summers and Tendai was still on her back. I couldn't send her away and keep her children. Children are to be left with their mother until they have seen seven seasons at least. There was no question of her going to her people with my children either. They are boys and I couldn't let them be raised by strangers who did not share their totem. I could not have given them to Maidei either. Taking children of that age away from their mother who is alive and well and giving them to another to look after is not done. Who would give or accept such a ruling? Maidei should have known that I could not send the child away.

Whatever made her go to the headman to ask for a dare and to make all those accusations and demands, only she herself knows. I didn't make her look after my children for nothing. How many pay a mother's cow for someone whose womb does not open? Was it not this that I was trying to avoid? Women! Nobody will ever know what goes on inside them. I should never have married. To think that I once swore never to marry, only to finish up with three women!

Ever since Maidei went away, the child does not stop complaining. "This child did this, this child did that …" What am I to do with them? They are children, are they not? If it is not the children, it is, "This neighbour did this to me, or said that to me." I don't want to hear about it.

Also, the child never stops accusing me of having loved Maidei. It's ten seasons since she left. How anyone can fight with a ghost is a mystery to me. When Maidei was here, she never asked why I loved her. Even though I have long since forgotten about her, I still have to answer to the child why I used to love Maidei. Sentiments again. If this is why we are here on this earth, to answer for our feelings, then the battle is already lost.

It is she who is more ashamed of me now. I am an old man and nothing is new to me any more. I do not cry if one points at me to say that I have a child for a wife. Of course, I have a child-wife. I am not the first one to do so and I shall not be the last.

"Did you hear that? They've just told me that I'm living with an old man and you are not doing anything about it. Do something! I want you to do something!"

But I am doing something, am I not? Keeping quiet in front of fools is doing something. Often, keeping quiet is harder and stronger than throwing a stone at somebody or arguing with them. But how to explain that?

My body is weak, my spirit is complaining and I would like it to rest. I have kept my promise to her mother and I have not sent her back. Now I would like Chenai to come for me. There is nothing to keep me here any longer. Tawa is married now and I have held his offspring in these arms of mine. I know that once I am gone he will return to look after everything. Wangi, I have put into Chenai's hands. Even though he's the oldest, I've always worried about him. Maybe it was too late for him when I took them away from my sister after their mother died. What choice did I have but to give the boys to my sister to look after? How was I to know that my own sister would starve my own children, her own nephews, as well as treat them like slaves? Wangi is lost for good. I do not think I shall ever hold one of his offspring in my arms.

Tawa did not marry for a long time because he was waiting for his older brother. But how can anybody marry if they never stay in one place? Even today, we do not know where Wangi is. Each time he's been home, I have tried to reason with him. It has always ended in a fight. I cannot put my hands on him any more. Is he going to wander the woods all his life? If it is Maidei disorienting Wangi for revenge, and she is already there with you, Chenai, I hope you will know how to protect your own. I count on you to do something about it. You cannot let your children down now after all you did to make sure they grew into men. Send Wangi home before I go so that I can make him give me his word he will marry. A maiden from a good family.

I do not have the energy to go on any longer. Even though Tawa is young, he will be able to look after his younger brothers and sisters. Tinashe and Tendai are ten and three and ten and two respectively. Soon they'll be adults. I worry about the one who is only a season for he will grow up without a father. Tawa will have to be there for him; the cattle pen is full enough for the three of them, so I know Tawa will be able to marry them off without struggling.

If the girls marry well, this means more cows. Each of the boys will receive danga from one sister and that sister will be his foster daughter in case of trouble. The two big boys will receive roora and look after the oldest two girls, Nyasha and Rumbi. The last boy will get the danga from Chido. Luckily the numbers were good to me. Three boys and three girls. Everything will be clear and there will be no fighting. With Tawa as the overall head, I do not have to worry. Only if Wangi came back to claim his birthright might there be problems. But I'm sure Tawa will know how to deal with his older brother. He has always known.

Tawa's wife I have nothing against, even though she is not of our people. She is respectful and beautiful. Though I don't know her well, she seems to have a good heart. She has already given Tawa a girl and a boy, whom they named after me, so that when I'm gone, I shall still be running around and they will not forget me. Wangi's son should have carried my name. He is the first born is he not? But fate is fate. "Give thanks for that you have swallowed; that in front of you still belongs to Musiki."

I must tell Tawa that if one day his lost brother ever returns and goes in a straight line, he should call his first daughter Chenai. That way, both of us will be remembered. I could let Tawa call his daughter Chenai, but it will not look good if ever his brother comes back. And him being the older of the two? Already Tawa has married before him. If only I could do something for Wangi before I go. I would have liked to divide the cattle between the two and give them each their responsibilities. As it is, it is better that I do not say anything. They will know what to do when the time comes. Tawa is capable of diffusing any situation. If he has any problems, he will go to Bikita and bring the others and, with their heads together, they will find a solution.

It is the child that I worry about. Will Tawa want to inherit her? She is still very young. Only two tens and five. Or maybe those from Bikita who never saw her with her nose running will want her. She looks attractive now, only she does not know it. Or Wangi, if he is still not married. That is if he ever comes for my funeral. If we ever find him. He is worse than a wild animal; a baboon knows to which clan he belongs. Wangi does not know any more. What are vasinamabvi giving them so they forget where they came from? The headman's son has long since disappeared. Three times they have brewed beer and done everything to bring him back. But there has been nothing. He's gone the way the rivers go. Our children have become rivers, which flow one way only and never come back to where they started. If one day the sun rose from the west, we should wonder no more. Musiki has his back to us and rags in his ears.

11

Chinongwa

I thought I could fall no further. I was already on the ground. Either I stayed there or stood up, but it was not to be.

It all started with the cousin from Bikita. How could I have suspected him? He was quiet and kept a respectful distance between us, hardly spoke to me. In any case, no man has ever been interested in me. I was disgusting but safe: I had just spent my married life trying in vain to make an old man like me and if not me, at least my body. I had tried everything. All the feminine tricks that Amaiguru had taught me had failed. Sekuru either looked at me with pity or he got angry and chased me away from him.

"I do not like libidinal women. When you were small, your parents must certainly have neglected to put a grinding stone on your chest to calm that ardour. Are you itching? Are you a bitch on heat? Be far from me; I am a human, not a bull on the hunt."

The more he chased me away, the more I chased him. I wanted him to at least acknowledge my existence. Why could he not even just once recognise me as a woman? Why pretend I was still a child? For how long was I going to remain a child?

Though I felt luckier than other women in that he had never laid his hand on me, sometimes I wished he did. I might have hit him back and gotten rid of some of the humiliation that I suffered. I could not stand his forever calm countenance that made me feel even more childish and stupid. It was easier to take when Amaiguru was there, for I believed she did something to make him prefer her. Though she'd given me to him, she had not renounced him. She was his wife; I was the reward that she'd offered him for his good behaviour. I could never be his wife as long as she was there. He would never love me in her stead.

But when she left, I could no longer go on blaming her. For a while I hoped, waiting for him to love and respect me. When he did not and I went out of my way to seduce him, he fought me all the way. He did not want to be captured. When I persisted, he turned his horns on me. He was not struggling any more but stood facing me, horns sharpened, ready to defend himself. If I got hurt in the process, he was not going to be responsible; he was only defending himself. His horns were words, their barbs as sharp as thorns. They sunk deep into me, widening the wound as they went until my heart was torn to tatters.

Even now, they still say that I was happy to see him die. There are some who even suggest that I killed him so that I could take the others in. I cannot explain to them what happened. They will never understand. Only Sekuru and I knew the rules of the game and only he and I were the players. There could be no third party.

At his funeral they wanted me to cry and tear my hair out. It reminded me of my mother's funeral when my eyes remained dry, but not for the same reasons. When my mother died, I realised that it was possible for me to be loved. Even though this was my mother, at the end of her life, the impact was immeasurable. There was no way I could cry after discovering this. I had said the most heartfelt goodbye to her and had wished her eternal peace. The love she had given me was glowing all around me and bathing me in warm colours. But I could not explain my beautiful secret to them. It would have spoiled everything. Anyway, they would not have understood.

While the secret at my mother's funeral was the most meaningful, this one was the emptiest. I knew that Sekuru had died so as to be rid of me. To tell me once and for all that he did not like me. He preferred to be dead than to love me. But how could I explain all that when, before he died, I had pretended that he loved me? Ever since Amaiguru went away, I pretended that he loved me. Even though he did everything to make me understand that he did not, when the other women asked me what is was like to be the only wife, I gave them the answers that they wanted to hear.

I did not care whether or not they found out one day. I was humiliated enough from carrying the truth inside me every day. Remembering what Amaiguru had told them when she sang me, I had to convince them things had changed, that it was her fault that he had not loved me then; that with her love potions she'd kept him away from me. In order to survive, I needed every day to hear that he cared for me. So in telling the others, I managed to tell myself what I needed to hear.

Most of them believed me. It is only normal that an old man should be proud of having a young wife. Even if I was the ugliest woman in the village, for him I should have been the most beautiful and he should have felt blessed. My problem was that he did not feel lucky. When Amaiguru left, he was forever visiting his relatives— except in the rainy season when we all spent our days in the field.

Whenever he came to my sleeping hut, he left me as soon as he was finished. The following day he looked ashamed of himself as if he had been thieving in the dark of the night, as if I was not his own wife, as if his cattle were not walking in the pens of my family.

He would be angry with me as if it had been my fault, as if I had dragged him in.

As for me, I would feel elated; I was triumphant. There was a gaiety in my step. I wanted to shout about it from the top of the mountain. I wanted to go and cry to the village, "Last night he came to my humble mat, last night I made him moan, the old baboon!" But then I had to suppress my jubilation so that in two or three nights he would be back to quench his thirsty loins—with me pretending it gave me no pleasure at all.

When he died, I knew it was his escape. He had won. I would never bother him again. He would never feel ashamed of himself again. He would no longer suffer from having to look me in the face the day afterwards.

At the funeral, while he lay on the mat and I sat at his feet and they were all crying, I was wondering if he still felt ashamed, if there was shame after death. He would never have touched me during the day, for then he would have been obliged to look at me. Even when he was drunk and would fall asleep right after, he made sure he quit me before it got light. It couldn't have been for the villagers, for I kept having children and he was praised for being such a bull. He took the credit with his head high as long as there were others around.

Did he do it just so he could have more children or because from time to time he needed it? He went away with the answer. Even if he were still here, the answer would still be in his chest. I would never have dared ask.

So I looked at his soulless body and searched the wall to see where his spirit was—I knew it was waiting for us to throw his body away, so it could finally free itself. I wanted to know whether he was feeling happier or if he still looked downcast. I wanted to know if there was any relief in his expression or even if he was looking triumphant?

While I looked for him and pondered this question, my eyes remained dry. A woman whose husband has just died does not have dry eyes. She weeps until she can weep no more. She faints and has water thrown on her to bring her back to the reality that her children are now orphans. She has to be both mother and father until the guva ceremony, when she has to choose—from her husband's totem cousins, brothers or sons from the other wives—which man inherits her and becomes her new husband and the father of the children. All these things should have been enough to make any woman cry. It is the wife's tears and suffering that should make a man's funeral memorable to everybody else. A woman who weeps well for her departed loved one brings tears into everybody's eyes. They should only need to look at her. When they go back to their homes after the burial, they should talk of nothing but the poor widow for many days to come. A new widow should look devastated, lost, sad, inconsolable, bordering on suicide. It should be the other women who comfort her and tell her to think of her beloved children.

If there are two or several wives, they should compete in fainting and weeping for their dead master. The one who weeps the most is the one who was most worthy of the master and really loved him. None should overdo it either, for the other mourners are not fools. They can detect real tears from false ones. They are there to see that justice is done. The vahosi does not have to throw herself in the dust like the younger wives. After all, she has the highest seat in the hierarchy and the seat demands some dignity. She is supposed to have suffered each time her husband brought a new wife to the family. She is older and wiser. In the end, even her husband will come to her when he can not take the heat because his younger wives are fighting or not talking to each other any more. She counsels, he follows. Because she, the first wife, had suffered so much, she nearly always looked older than him. And because the death of her husband was not going to deprive her of much more than a friend, who was not very loyal, she didn't have to pull her hair out or put ashes on her face.

Here I was, an only wife whose husband had sacrificed his other wife, and I was not rolling myself in dust and spreading ash on my face. Twice, not once, the headman's wife came to tell me to cry more, otherwise people were going to talk. Even Tete Shorai kept throwing me these looks. There was no mistaking what she was trying to tell me.

As long as I wondered whether or not he was happy leaving me, I couldn't cry. I was also gripped with fear that somehow the mourners would conclude that he had died because he didn't love me; because he was ashamed of sleeping with me and placing his seed in me. I kept watch over him for I was convinced he would rise up and tell them that he needed to be free of me and had gone to join his dead wife. I didn't mind him joining her; I minded him joining Amaiguru. Since I didn't know whether or not Amaiguru was dead, I feared he was going to join her. I could hear her mocking laughter and I felt as naked as I did the day she sang me; and while I searched for his shadow on the wall and listened to Amaiguru's laughter, my eyes remained dry, and the village started humming with disapproval. It was a memorable funeral for my lack of tears.

It was not as if I had a heart of stone; I knew how to cry. Out of the ten children that I had had, seven are walking today. The other three I had given back to Musiki.

The first child, a son, lived for three weeks only. Even though Amaiguru was there and did everything she could, I never understood why he died. He looked well and was drinking his milk. Then one day, without warning, he wouldn't take the breast. I did not know what to do. I cried to make him, but he wouldn't listen. I asked him, I begged and cajoled, but he refused. At first he stared at me and then he closed his eyes and cried softly. Then he began hicupping ceaselessly. I didn't understand. Nobody could tell me. When he stopped breathing, there was nothing else to do. I wanted to keep him for a while, just a day, just in case he came alive again, but they told me it was no use. Why had nobody, but nobody, ever told me that we bear children only to see them die? We can't do anything for them. They're suffering and we sit and watch them. We cannot even share their pain, or assume it and suffer for them. I'd gladly have taken his pain and waited for him to leave this world peacefully. But no, he had to go the hard way, even though he was just a baby.

The second child to die, I never even held in my arms because I was too ill to know what was happening. She was the fourth child. A few days later, when I had recovered, I was shown where they had placed her. She was the price I paid for singing Amaiguru.

When the third baby died, even though I had already buried two and lived in fear of losing others, I wasn't expecting it as she was already walking and talking. She was even able to tell me where she was hurting, but once more I sat and watched her suffering. She died in my arms. For a while I walked around as if I were dead, asking myself why I was filling the wetlands with my babies. Why was I being punished? I still see my children and cry for them. Would my destiny have changed if I had kept them all? Should I complain even though I still have the seven that are living? Yes, I think so, because they were mine. I was given them only to have them taken away. I also cry for the living ones that I don't have with me now. There's a blank space where they should be sitting.

Yes I'm still angry with him, but I still cry for Baba Chitsva, though no one will believe me. Maybe it was because I didn't cry enough at Baba Chitsva's funeral, that Cousin Mahora didn't think I suffered. But why did I trust him? Because I couldn't be a target; I was repulsive, wasn't I? Until the deed was done, violation had nothing to do with me; it only happened to desirable women, those with trembling thighs.

Yet the very same women who laughed at me, Mapfupa the ugly, Mapfupa the 'gift' that none of their men would ever have accepted, now blame me. They accuse me of using witchcraft to ensnare them. Otherwise, how can they explain why their husbands weren't disgusted by me. After Amaiguru sang me, they were even more convinced that if an old man like Baba Chitsva wouldn't want me, their wonderful husbands wouldn't either. Perhaps their husbands assured them I was repellent.

So, though I was a new widow, I wasn't a threat to anyone. That's why Mahora, the cousin from Bikita, was a shock. He hardly ever looked at me. The cousin had been in the village for just two days. He was family; nobody feared events like that especially before the guva ceremony. Our family was still in mourning. Hadn't he come to consult with Tawa about the ceremony? Later, he would claim it was because he had drunk too much. If Tawa hadn't gone back to town to fetch his property so as to finally settle home after his father's death, who knows.

I wouldn't be sitting here would I?

The headman had invited the village to his home for he'd brewed some beer to appease his thirsty dead grandfather, who was giving him a lot of bad luck by letting the hyenas kill his cattle. Since Mahora, the cousin, drank, I informed him that there was a feast at the headman's. He spent the whole day there. I only went in the morning, just to show my face. In the evening I sent one of the girls, Rumbi, to call the cousin for supper, but he said he'd already eaten at the headman's. Since he was sleeping in the cooking hut, I prepared his mat and blankets and went to sleep in my hut.

Tinashe and Tendai, who had seen ten and three and ten and two summers, went to sleep in their hut; and the girls, Nyasha and Rumbi, who had seen nine and seven, went to theirs while I went to sleep with the two smallest, Chido and Tatenda, who were three and one.

All I remember was feeling a hand on my face and, for a while, I couldn't breathe. I couldn't tell who it was and he didn't speak. If only the children had been a bit older, they might have been woken by the struggling. If only one of them had even cried, the cousin might have taken fright. When I finally screamed it was too late. I just managed to hold on to his coat that he slipped out of trying to escape. That's how I knew who it was.

Straight away, with the coat, I went to the headman. He was not yet sleeping as there was still Baba Mashava the alcoholic, who was just about to leave.

Even now, four seasons later, I still don't see how I could have come out of it clean. If I hadn't gone to the headman, I would have been accused of complicity. Because I went, I got myself into worse trouble, which I couldn't have foreseen. The headman called the cousin and he confessed in front of the headman. He swore in front of headman, Baba Mashava the alcoholic, and the headman's wife, that he would come to the guva ceremony. So, the headman decided that it was in nobody's interest to make the affair public. Things were bad enough because he had dared touch me before the cleansing ceremony. The headman decided that he would have to pay two head of cattle to appease Baba Chitsva's spirit—but that would be afterwards and within the family. He was, after all, a Chitsva. The headman thought that if handled properly, discreetly, this violation could be hushed up.

It seemed prudent at the time, and all present agreed. The headman told me that on the day of guva, after the night feast and dancing, once the brothers and Chitsva cousins who were eligible to inherit me were assembled, I was to act as if nothing had happened, and to give the spear to cousin Mahora so as to legalise everything. After the ceremony, Mahora would then kill an ox and ask excuses from his dead cousin, my husband, before touching me officially. Only Tawa was to be told of what had actually occurred.

Mahora slept at the headman's and was ordered to depart the next morning, leaving his axe and coat behind as proof that he had wronged. If he didn't turn up for the ceremony, then the headman would tell everyone what he'd done and the punishment would be severe.

It was only the next day that the significance of it all sank in. I had been dirtied, and now at the age of two tens and six, I was going to be married off to someone I didn't know who had already violated me. Would I ever be free? I had met Mahora only twice before the funeral of Baba Chitsva. I didn't know what to expect of him. I knew he had a wife in Bikita. He was younger than Baba Chitsva. His father had been Baba Chitsva's brother. So he was a totem brother to Sekuru and would now be my next husband whether I liked it or not. Though I had feared being inherited, I had thought that at least this time I would have a choice. If I did not want them, I was not obliged to marry them. I could give the spear to Tinashe, my oldest son, though everybody was advising me to choose someone for protection's sake. I also knew that nobody, especially the women, wanted to have a manless woman living in the village. They wanted me to be stowed away with someone. Shamhu, who had come to stay with me after Sekuru's funeral, felt strongly I would be better off with a protector and had been advising me whom to choose.

My problem was that I was convinced none of my husband's totem brothers or cousins would want me. However, all those who are eligible are obliged to sit on the mat and wait to receive the spear, whether or not they like the widow. How humiliating it would be if, when I gave one of them the spear, he would pass it on. I couldn't bring myself to tell Shamhu of my fears. I implied them, but she did not pick up on my hints. She sounded as if all the men would be fighting for me. Was she blind?

I had nightmares about the spear being passed from cousin to cousin, from uncle to nephew, until I had given it to them all and they had all refused me. Why would anyone accept me when Sekuru had refused me all his life? I'd never heard of a widow who was refused by all, but then neither had I heard of a young wife who repulsed her elderly husband.

If that happened, that would be the end of me. I would never hold my head up again. I lost a lot of sleep with the anxiety of it all. Now the cousin's act had eliminated the problem and my fear of embarrassment. But I had a new question: if Sekuru had always found me disgusting, why had his cousin wanted me? Was his act sent from above, one determined by the ancestors, or was it a conscious choice? Perhaps it was simply animal lust? Should I now be relieved that I was not going to be refused in front of everybody? At one moment I felt relief that I would no longer have to go down the row of aspiring husbands laying the spear at the feet of each; but in the next moment, I felt so unclean, so soiled that I scrubbed myself in scalding water with boiled muzumbani leaves.

The guva ceremony was still a long way off. So for at least two moons, I was gripped by anxiety that I might be with child. It was one thing to hide that I had been violated, but quite another to explain how I found myself pregnant. The headman's wife was the only person with whom I could talk and I was grateful. If I'd been left all alone, I would surely have gone mad. But, as the days passed and it seemed that I was not with child, I began to regret that I had told the headman.

If I'd kept quiet, I would still be free to choose whom I wanted, and I would choose Tawa, but just as protector and children's overseer. I would lay the spear at his feet but refuse to wash his face, thereby refusing the four feet under the covers. Tawa would not have insisted. I would then have my liberty and I would be safe for they would not do to me what had been done to Sekuru Taguta's wife. If anybody were to smash down my door in the middle of the night, they would have to face Tawa, for I would be under his protection. But now, all because of cousin Mahora, I no longer had this choice. I was simply going to become his second wife. I did not know whether he was going to take me to Bikita or whether

I was going to stay where I was and he would come to me from time to time. I knew there would be no answer until after the guva ceremony. Mahora had been forbidden to set foot in the village until then. So I waited.

12

Chinongwa

Unspeakable things happened after cousin Mahora violated me. Events became so embroiled I wasn't sure if I was dead or alive, asleep or awake, going or coming. I couldn't face the ceremony as if nothing had happened. Just thinking of his violation tied my stomach in knots and made me weep. I felt I couldn't go through with the ceremony; I felt it would be physically impossible. Walking, eating and sleeping became almost insuperable chores and the event loomed like a precipice that dared me to climb it.

As the day of kurova guva approached and more people arrived for it, fear made me numb and I felt as if I was suffocating. How could I extract myself from this impossible trap? To avoid scandal, the headman had made us swear to seal our mouths. So all those present—that is, the headman's wife, Baba Mashava the alcoholic, and I—had each touched his spear while swearing, "Cut off my lips should I divulge this sacred secret." Baba Mashava was warned not to tell his wife and I was warned not to tell Shamhu.

Though Baba Mashava didn't tell his wife, he certainly remembered what had happened. If he hadn't been at the headman's when I went to report the cousin's act, what would have happened? I know it is no use asking myself this question, but I do every day. So, when Baba Mashava violated me, he did so without shame as he watched me wipe the blood and grass off my face, as I told him I was going to tell the headman.

"I would like to see the headman believe you. Go ahead—tell him! But don't forget I shall tell him my side of the story."

"How can you do this to me? And in my mourning period! The dare will decide what to do with you. I have nothing to say to you. And Tawa will be here soon."

"Do you have witnesses? And if I say I never touched you? Or if I say you arranged to meet me here? If I tell them that it wasn't the first time that we've been together? And am I the first one? No! Do you honestly think the headman will believe a woman coming for the second time to tell him that she has been forced? Run now. Go! Run! Go and tell the woods, the sky, and don't forget the rivers; they will be jealous if you don't give them the news. I'm not allowed to tell anybody about the cousin who came onto your mat, what do I get in exchange? You are missing your old man, are you not? And here I give you a taste of a real man and you don't appreciate it. Go to the headman and see if he believes you. Run! He can't wait to hear your news."

If only Baba Nhongo had not drowned himself that very morning, the headman or his wife might have been at home when I called. And who knows, today I would perhaps have my children with me.

Instead, the whole village was at the riverside trying to retrieve the body, so I went home to heat some water, scrub myself and change my dress. I felt dirty and worthless. But most of all I felt lost. Maybe what Baba Mashava had said was true. There was going to

222

be a big dare and they would believe him not me. And if they did, what would happen to me?

When I went to the riverside, Baba Mashava was already there. He ignored me as if nothing had happened. To make it worse, we could not find Baba Nhongo's body for two whole days. We made a fire by the river and the best swimmers took turns to dive in search of it, even during the night; but to no avail. Finally, the body was fished out by the spirit medium, who had been shown where he was during her sleep; but it was another two days before he was buried.

By then it was too late to tell them what had happened four days earlier. Ever since I'd told him about the cousin in Bikita, I knew that the headman looked askance at me. He never said a word but then he did not have to. I knew he blamed me for what had happened. His wife told me not to mind, that his behaviour was driven by the worry that the secret might come out before the ceremony. Every time he saw me he was reminded of it.

So Baba Mashava did what he wanted with me in exchange for his not telling anyone about the cousin in Bikita. Either we were seen or he boasted about it, but one day he brought me one of his neighbours of the east side and told me that he also knew and I had to keep him quiet. I kept him quiet. After all, what did it matter now? Whether it was one, two or three of them was not going to change anything. When they brought a third and a fourth one, I didn't ask questions. I didn't even care whether the village knew or not. The only thing I cared about were my children and I cried every time I thought of what was happening to me and that one day they would find out.

When at the end of the harvest period I could not take their demands any more, I wished that the village or someone knew and would put a stop to it. At least two or three times a week, I had demands made of me. By then, they were coming to my house to ask me for it on the pretence that they were bringing firewood to brew the beer for the feast. That their wives were also coming to help brew beer for the ceremony did not dissuade them. While I kept one quiet inside the hut, the others kept watch outside by pretending to cut logs.

Either because I couldn't stop crying or because someone had heard or seen something, one of the old women preparing the beer asked me if something was wrong. I could have said that it was the coming ceremony and having to choose a new husband that was making my tears flow; or told her that I was crying for my lost husband, but instead, I poured it all out. As I spoke, I realised that I had been waiting all along for someone to ask me what was wrong, so that the nightmare would end.

There was consternation, indignation, disbelief, recoil, shame and anger. Depending on who it was, these feelings were directed at me, the cousin from Bikita, the headman, or the blackmailers. We were just three days away from the ceremony. Though nearly everybody called for dignity and secrecy, by nightfall the scandal had made the rounds of the village and travelled further, and as it did so, juices were added here and there.

There must have been so much talk of the forthcoming ceremony that on the day of the feast, people started arriving well before sunset. They wanted to have a good look at me before it got too dark. It was the biggest guva ceremony I had ever witnessed. Because all the people couldn't fit in one hut, it was decided to have three different sets of drums: one set in the cooking hut, one in Baba Chitsva's sleeping hut and another one outside. All night long, these drums called out to each other, competed with each other and sent the revellers round and round in mad and drunken circles. The drummers sent the tempo rising and falling as their hands dictated. The dancing bodies rose and fell outside and within the two huts until the early morning when more than half of the revellers lay sprawled in all degrees of consciousness, in all kinds of postures, and snored to the music still playing inside the two huts. Baba Chitsva's spirit had thus been brought back home to protect those he had left behind.

Once more, I was asking myself whether or not, after all that had happened, he was going to bother to protect me. What did he think of me now? Was I still his wife? Had he forsaken me because, instead of mourning for him, I had let myself be violated?

As to the ceremony of selecting a husband among the eligible cousins, it was decided instead to hold a dare where my blackmailers were called to answer for their crimes. They did not deny them. They were ordered to pay two head of cattle per man as damages to Tawa, who was now the head of the family. The cousin from Bikita was also ordered to pay damages to Tawa, who refused to accept, saying that it was up to Baba Chitsva, now that his spirit had been brought back into the family, to deal with his cousin as he wished.

I was given back to my people, who were told in no uncertain terms that I was not fit to live in the Chitsva home. With the urging of those present, I was ordered to leave the home of Chitsva, taking with me Tatenda only. He had seen two seasons at the time. Chido, even though she had only seen four seasons, was not allowed to come with me and I was not allowed to return to see my other children. They were not to visit me either. What I had done, or what had been done to me, made me forfeit my children forever. Tatenda was to be given back to Tawa as soon as he had seen seven seasons.

My family was too ashamed to make any demands. They could not even raise their heads when they heard the men who had blackmailed me come forward, one after the other, to give evidence of what they had done to me. Tete Shorai has still never spoken to me about it. We all pretend that it never happened. Only strangers whisper the scandal.

In normal divorce circumstances, I would have been allowed to take Chido. Had she seen seven seasons? No, only four, but they said that if I took her I would teach her my manners. Did I rape myself? When Tawa and Shamhu tried to argue against them, all the village women jumped on them. They wanted to get back at me. Unbelievably, they were jealous. You would have thought I'd dragged their men on to my mat crying. Now they didn't feel so superior. No, I was a bewitching temptress who used snake-skin oil to entice their men. That these same men had made public confessions were ignored. Their husbands were innocent victims.

And now they give my children to Tawa's wife to raise. Is a streetlight woman more respectable than me? Don't we know what she was doing in Harare? The vasinambvi do not allow men to live with their wives when they work in town. With whom do all these men relieve themselves? Did I say anything when Tawa brought her home? After all, who was I to say what I thought. Sekuru fell for her. If I'd known Tawa was going to send me away like he did, I would've told him what I thought of his letter-writing, hair-plaiting, clean-handed, streetlight wife.

Before his wife came, Tawa had to buy a bed for her. What is wrong with a reed mat? She washes her clothes in hot water, not at the river like us. She tells us our water has germs. When Tawa goes to Harare to work for mutero, she writes letters to him. Who knows what she says about my children in those letters. She plaits her hair in a manner that nobody has ever seen before. There are some in the village who are even copying her plaits. And they all flock to her so that she can write letters for them. She prays to the Musiki of vasinamabvi. I never fell for that. Even though I have never been to the city, it is not hard to recognise the leisure girl that she once was. One does not marry a woman one meets in the city. One should marry people from one's own village. People who speak the same way. Poor Tawa was enticed. He even went to the end of the world to give roora to her people.

226

Now, what good manners is a woman like that going to teach my daughters? To be leisure girls? But Tawa is blinded by that plaited hair and those soft hands.

I would like my girls to get married as soon as possible because Tawa's wife is using them to clean for her, to bring her water from the well, to wash her clothes in hot water they have to bring from the river. They weed her fields and cut wood for her while she writes letters and plaits her hair. They are her husband's brothers and sisters and she should give them the same respect that she gives to her husband, but instead she sits there and gives them orders. They do the dirty work because she must not make her hands dirty. They're the ones who should be giving her orders. They think I don't know about any of this, but words cross rivers and mountains. They float like pollen and settle into my ears, which are always open.

A maiden who works for the kneeless! What for? Does she pay mutero? I'm still looking for an answer. A maiden with parents and family who just ups and goes to look after children of vasinamabvi. What do her parents think? Are there no men in her family? What are they doing while she works for mutero? How many men have tears in their eyes when they leave their families for work? If the vasinambvi did not make men pay mutero, who would leave for the unknown instead of staying with their people? She is a street-light if ever there was one.

My children will come to me when the time comes. I carried them in my womb for nine moons. I am their mother and she is not. They will come to me. A calf may not know what lies beyond the hills but it knows where it came from. They are attached to me by the birth cord. Nobody can change that.

After being here four seasons, I have stopped crying. I have found peace even though my own people watch me in fear because they think I shall take their men from them. And they pity me because I do not have a man of my own. They do not know it is I

227

who pities them. I do not care that they whisper when they see me go by, or that they encourage their children not to respect me.

When they sent me back, I was full of shame and would have preferred to stay in the Chitsva family. I would have preferred to be inherited by one of the men. Now I think it was a blessing in disguise. I have finally found my independence. While in the beginning, I was lost, not knowing what to do every morning because no one was giving me orders, now I savour this freedom. The independence I fought so hard for, I would never have found in the Chitsva family. Amaiguru could not have given it to me either; she herself was not free.

Tatenda was on the breast when I arrived. I'm grateful for having him with me. In one more season his people want me to take him back. He would have seen the stipulated seven seasons by then. I have decided that I shall not return him. I shall wait for them to come and drag him away from me. I am treating the days that I have him with me as a stolen and forbidden pleasure. I am living them intensely.

As to the little one, she belongs to me and nobody else. I called her Chikomborero because at the end of the day, regardless of all that happened, she is a blessing to me. No man has any claim on her. She is mine and I do not fear losing her. Whose seed begot her, I shall never know. She is a product of my womb, but unlike the others, she belongs to me. Every day when I look at her, it feels like a balm being applied to my wounded soul.

At first I refused to accept what life had dealt me. I said that my load was too heavy. But, with time, and as I look around me, I decided that one will never know the weight of one's neighbour's load. Maybe if I were to carry it, I might ask for mine back. Only that one who carries it knows its weight.

As to those of my natal home who look down on me, I say ushingi, courage. I intend to settle and live my life here. There are those who won't talk to me because I am dirty, and those who

228

would like me to be chased out of the village. I bear no grudges. From their lofty pedestals they have judged and found me guilty. I shall leave them to their occupations. When someone new to hate or drive out arrives, they will forget all about me and concentrate on the new victim. They complained when Tichafa gave me part of the land which they feel should be for Ngoni, the oldest boy. But Ngoni has not yet come back. Maybe he never will. If and when he does, they'll chase me away. I shall take my children, pack my belongings and go to other lands. Far from them. And I shall tell them, like Amaiguru did to her people, not to bother burying me.

Soon I shall have cows of my own. When my sister Muraswa died, she left her mother's cows in her husband's pens. Recently, her oldest son came to ask me to accept the cows. Muraswa must be smiling down on me. Five head, they told me.

I shall enjoy as much as I can those five head, for my sister died without ever enjoying anything in her life. We all know she died from the beatings. He swept her yard every morning before leaving so as to see who visited in his absence. When he came back he would inspect all the footprints. If there were any that he did not recognise, Muraswa had to answer for it. When he felt his last days approaching, he was seized with the fear that when he was gone Muraswa could be inherited by one of his family. An unbearable thought, so he made sure she died before him. Nobody was going to touch his young wife. A dog has more freedom than my sister had. She was not allowed to visit her parents or me. None of us were allowed to visit her. She was not allowed to have friends in the village. She was not even permitted to talk to her co-wives. They were a bad influence, he told her. She could talk to the vahosi only.

The one thing he could not take from her was her mother's cows. I hope my sister feels avenged and will make them prosper in my hands. Now that he is also dead, I shall wait a respectable period and then go and look for my sister's daughters. I hope they are happy with whomsoever they married. Anyway, nobody could be as evil as their father. Muraswa's load was definitely heavier than mine. When I think of her life, I'm ashamed that I ever complained about mine. Maybe I should go to her grave and break a gourd of beer and tell her to rise and return to fight. But then maybe I should not. Muraswa, in her fury, might come back and harm her own children. They are her husband's family and they carry his totem, after all.

Still, once I have my own cattle, I shall be my own woman. The little land I have is enough for two children, but it won't be enough if the others come to join me. I shall have to move though I do not know where. People say there are some headmen who now refuse to give people land. I don't think it's true. How can anyone refuse the other land? Nobody owns it. If we were to become like vasinamabvi, then that will be the end of us. People say the kneeless do not share land and will kill you if you walk on theirs. Or they ask for mutero for living on their land or letting your cattle graze. How can that be true?

I know one should not build a pen before the cattle arrive, but I know deep inside me that one day my children will come to me. Maybe the older boys, Tinashe and Tendai, will not, but the younger ones will. I know Tinashe is now married and has a son. I am a grandmother. Soon Tendai will marry. He has already seen ten and six summers. Tinashe was not much older when he married. They say his wife is beautiful. I'm sure I shall see her one day. The two boys were at the dare about the blackmail so maybe they are ashamed of me, and due to what they saw and heard, they will not come to live with me.

But the girls, once they are married, will look for me. Anyway, Tawa has to call me when their husbands bring the roora. Whatever he thinks of me, even though they banished me away from their home, no roora can be given in the absence of the mother. And Nyasha has already seen ten and four summers and is ready to be married. Rumbi has seen ten and two and is also ready to be married. I already had children by that age. There is nothing to stop them if they want to. But Tawa is making them go to school. As I have said, I have now seen four seasons since I came back to my father's home. I have learnt to depend on my own resources, to be my own master and mistress, my own mother and father. I have learnt to make decisions without first going to ask Amaiguru, Sekuru, the headman's wife or Shamhu. It was hard at first, but with time I have grown stronger.

Now that I have the choice to marry whoever I wish the idea seems preposterous. To think that I used to dream of choosing a man for myself! My only dream that's ever come true, and one I relish with a vengeance, is being able to whistle like a man. I was told a woman fit to be married should not whistle. I don't want to be married so the more they point at me, the louder I whistle. My load is still heavy on my head, but my heart is light, for I know, like the sun, that I shall rise every morning. Be it cloudy, cold or wet, I shall not fail to rise. And I shall whistle as loudly as I like. To me, it is the sound of freedom.

GLOSSARY

Mai	Mother
Maiguru	older sister, senior co-wife, senior wife of one's father or wife of older brother
Ambuya	Grandmother
Baba	Father or Mister
chigadzamapfihwa	woman given to widower in replacement of own or father's sister who has just died
chikuva	platform inside the cooking hut-used to hold the earthenware pots and sometimes as altar to send prayers to *Musiki* or family spirits
chinyarara	don't cry
chirongo	necked clay pot used for carrying water or brewing beer
danga	the cattle herd paid as bride dowry
dare	village court
dhuku	headscarf
dombo	hearthstone
dovi	peanut butter
dzoka	come back
godo	bone or jealousy
gumbeze rMai	the mother's blanket i.e. a blanket given to the bethrothed's mother at the *roora* ceremony
guva	grave-hitting
hari	clay cooking pot
hozi	elevated hut for grain storage
hute	fruit of *mukute* tree (*syzygium cordatum*)

ishwa	flying termite
kneeless	colonialists (they looked kneeless because of the trousers they wore)
kubarirwa	literally 'born for': a custom by which a family pledges an unborn daughter to a creditor
kumusha	(at) home
kurova guva	all-night dancing and drinking ceremony held one wet season after an adult person's death. It is supposed to bring back the dead, the spirit that's been wandering aimlessly. Once home, the spirit will protect the clan into the future.
mahewu	non-alcoholic drink from sadza
mahumbwe	organised make-believe house that was played just after the harvest, children formed families and cooked outside, usually behind the village
mainini	step-mother or mother's younger sister
mapfupa	bones
mapodzi	a sweet soft pumpkin that matures soon after the rainy season
masadza	beer brewed from the leftover sadza eaten at a funeral; and drunk a week afterwards.
mashura	'the impossible'
masungiro	a welcoming ceremony for a bride just before the birth of her first child
matengu	huge handless baskets used at harvest and as a vehicle of measurement
mazhanje	fruit of the *muzhanje* tree (*uapaca kirkiana*)
mbira	small many-keyed musical instrument
mhepo	evil winds
M'kuwasha	son-in-law, or sister's husband
mombe yeumai	mother's cow
muchakata	wild fruit tree whose shoots are used as a toothbrush (*parinari curatellifolia*)
mugodhi	mine
mugodo	tree with soft leaves (*combretum apiculatum*)
Mukoma	elder sibling (used as sign of respect)
munyai	a go-between in a *roora* ceremony

Muroora	daughter-in-law
muroyi	witch
murume	man
murungu	white person
musasa	an African tree, also known as zebrawood, widely used for firewood (*brachystegia spiciformis*)
Musiki	the Creator (God)
mutero	an annual tax the colonial government levied on adult black males over the age of fifteen
muzumbani	shrub (*lippia javanica*)
mwanasikana	girl-child or daughter
n'anga	healer and diviner
ngozi	haunting spirit, usually from a murdered person
nhengeni	wild sour plum (from *ximenia caffra*)
rapoko	tiny grained millet that makes a reddish porridge
roora	dowry paid for the bride
rukoto	beer brewed by every household to ask for good rains
sadza	stiff porridge from ground maize, millet, sorghum or rice
Sekuru	Grandfather or maternal uncle
Tete	paternal aunt
tezvara	father-in-law or wife's brother
tsubvu	olive-like fruit (from *vitex Mombassa* and *payos*)
tsvimborume	unmarried childless old bachelor—set in his ways
tswanda	handless basket
urimbo	latex used as birdlime
ushingi	courage
vahosi	first wife in a polygamous marriage
vakabarirwa	They were blessed
vakomana	boys
Vakuru	Elder
varungu	whites
vasikana	girls
vasinamabvi	the kneeless i.e. white people
woman king	Queen Victoria (in this case)
zvirongo	plural of *chirongo*

Other books by Spinifex Press

The Screaming of the Innocent
Unity Dow

We are looking for a man with a hard heart; a heart of stone; a heart of a real man.

One afternoon, a 12-year-old girl goes missing. The local police tell her mother and the villagers she has been taken by a wild animal. Five years later, a young government worker finds evidence of foul play in the disappearance. So begins the struggle for justice and retribution against the forces of corruption. Challenging the romantic representations of Africa, former High Court judge Unity Dow tackles issues of human rights for women and girls in Botswana in this brilliant but disturbing novel.

Dow's writing is elegant and cadenced – she has the kind of earthy immediacy that transports you into her world and keeps you there.
—Cameron Woodhead, *The Age*

ISBN 9781876756208

Juggling Truths
Unity Dow

2006 Finalist, Percy Fitzpatrick Prize for Children's Literature

Go to the past with me, so you can take the past to the future …

Juggling Truths portrays the childhood of Monei Ntuka in a village in Botswana. This is an extraordinary journey through the conflicting versions of the truth that shape Monei's life—the truths of the colonisers, the churches and of her own people, like her wise storytelling grandmother. There is tension between the old and new ways, which Unity Dow recreates with telling insight and gentle humour. This is a world where the truths of the missionaries and the witchdoctors jostle with those of the generations of women.

Guileless yet clever, courageous and fiercely concerned for justice.
—Debra Adelaide, *The Sydney Morning Herald*

ISBN 9781876756383

Everything Good Will Come
Sefi Atta

Winner of the Wole Soyinka Prize for Literature in Africa

This is a powerful and eloquent story of a young woman's coming of age. It is 1971, and Nigeria is under military rule and 11-year-old Enitan Taiwo is tired of waiting for school to start. Will her mother, who has become deeply religious since the death of Enitan's brother, allow her to be friends with the new girl next door, Sheri Bakare? The two girls' paths traverse this novel—one manipulates the traditional system, the other attempts to defy it.

A literary masterpiece ... It portrays the complicated society and history of Nigeria through ... brilliant prose.

—*World Literature Today*

... a beautifully paced stroll in the shoes of a woman growing up in a country struggling to find its post-Independence identity ...

—*Times Literary Supplement*

ISBN 9781876756666

A Bit of Difference
Sefi Atta

At thirty-nine, Deola Bello, is a dissatisfied Nigerian expat in London, working in finance for an international charity. When her job takes her back to Nigeria in time for her father's five-year memorial service, she finds herself turning her scrutiny inward. In Nigeria, she encounters changes in her family and in the urban landscape of her home, and new acquaintances who offer unexpected possibilities. Deola's journey is as much about evading others' expectations to get to the heart of her frustration as it is about exposing the differences between foreign images of Africa and the realities of contemporary Nigerian life.

Atta's splendid writing sizzles with wit and compassion. This is an immensely absorbing book.

—Chika Unigwe, author of *On Black Sisters Street*

ISBN 9781876756994

If you would like to know more about
Spinifex Press, write to us for a free catalogue, visit our
website or email us for further information
on how to subscribe to our monthly newsletter.
Spinifex Press
PO Box 105
Mission Beach QLD 4852
Australia
www.spinifexpress.com.au
women@spinifexpress.com.au